WITH DAD ALONE

WITH DAD ALONE

JERROLD BEIM

ILLUSTRATED BY DON SIBLEY

NEW YORK

HARCOURT, BRACE AND COMPANY

COPYRIGHT, 1954, BY JERROLD BEIM

LIBRARY OF CONGRESS CATALOG CARD NUMBER: 54-8567

PRINTED IN THE UNITED STATES OF AMERICA

For Grandma, Jacques and Jeanette

WITH DAD ALONE

ONE

They were ready to leave right after breakfast. All three of them, Bruce, Robby and Mr. Madison, were sitting in the front of the car.

"Be sure to telephone us when you reach home," Grandpa said from the curb. Grandma looked as if she were going to cry and Bruce tried not to notice it. He felt mixed up enough about going home after the summer here and if Grandma cried he would be more sad than glad.

"Are the bikes tied on real good?" Robby asked, glancing toward the back of the car with concern.

"You know we're the best bicycle-tier-upers in the world!" Dad smiled. "Are we all set? Let's go!"

"Good-bye! Good-bye!" the boys called and waved. The car drove along the street which was lined with houses and trees that were older than either Grandpa or Grandma.

3

The three Madisons looked alike. Bruce was ten, going on eleven and Robby was seven. They had the same flashing dark eyes as Dad, and the kind of smiles that turned up more at one corner than the other. Bruce's hair was lighter, however, more like his mother's had been.

It took several hours to drive from this town, called Lindsay, to Brockton where they lived.

The car reached the highway soon, passing places and signs that Bruce and Robby knew well.

"Will we get home in time to play with the Dickersons?" Bruce asked.

"Oh, yes!" Dad assured him. "I saw Jimmy before I left the house on Friday. I told him you'd be back this afternoon."

That was one good thing about going home, Bruce thought. He would be seeing Jimmy again.

The Dickerson family lived next door and Bruce had played with Jimmy ever since they had both been little kids together. There were four Dickerson children in all, Linda who was a year younger than Jimmy, Phil who was Robby's best friend, and Taffy who was a little baby.

At about a quarter to twelve Dad said, "Let's start looking for a good place to have lunch."

"There's the frozen custard stand!" Robby exclaimed. "Can't we eat there, Dad, can't we?"

Bruce was delighted as the car slowed down before the stand that had a big, make-believe ice cream cone perched on top.

They had hamburgers first and then decided on their cones.

"I want chocolate!" Robby announced, but Bruce's favorite was vanilla. Dad decided to take chocolate, too.

"I think I can manage to eat this and drive at the same time," he said as they started back to the car.

Luckily the cones were wrapped in paper napkins, or else Robby would have made quite a mess of himself. Dad asked Bruce to help Robby wipe his face after the cones were finished.

"I can do it myself!" Robby insisted, but that wasn't quite true and Bruce completed the job for him.

Bruce felt excited when they finally reached Brockton. There was the airplane plant where Dad worked, the long, low building with the high, wire fence around it. Bruce was very proud of his father being an important engineer, helping to build wonderful planes.

Soon they were riding through the downtown

5

section, past Hemple's Department Store and the Tivoli Theatre and on to Clayton Park.

"Can we go rowing sometime, Dad, before the lake freezes up for the winter?" Bruce asked.

"Perhaps!" Dad smiled. "I can't promise definitely—"

"There's our school!" Robby exclaimed. "Grandma gave me a new pencil box for next term."

"And—and there's our street—" Bruce said. He suddenly felt scared, not certain at all whether he was glad to be home.

The house didn't look any different, white with green trim, a flagstone walk dividing the lawn into two neat squares.

"The grass doesn't look too good. I'm afraid I neglected it over the summer," Dad said as he drove the car into the driveway.

Robby was in a hurry to get out of the car but Dad made each of them carry something, taking the heaviest suitcases himself.

Bruce walked slowly, hesitantly, toward the door. Often, before the summer, Dad had taken Robby and him on an errand after dinner. They would come home, the three of them alone, like this. When they entered the house Mom would be waiting in the living room for them. What if she were there

6

now, Bruce thought, but no—he knew that couldn't be, because Mom had died just at the beginning of the summer.

"There're some letters in the mailbox, I can see them!" Robby said, stretching up on his toes.

Dad took them out. "Just some bills," he said, and then Bruce, glancing next door, suddenly saw the Dickersons.

They were all coming out of their house, Jimmy, Linda, Phil—all the children except Taffy who was a baby.

"Hello—hello—we're back!" Robby started to run toward Phil but Bruce didn't move.

Jimmy and Linda didn't move either. They just smiled at Bruce. They hadn't seem him since his mother died. They were looking at him now as if they felt shy and didn't know what to say.

"Hello there!" Dad called to them. "I think Bruce wants to go inside for a while but he'll be out soon."

They entered the house now and Bruce stood in the middle of the living room, motionless, almost afraid to look around.

"It's awfully dark in here. Why don't you pull back the drapes?" Dad said to him.

Bruce walked to the window, tugged at the cord, and sunlight flooded the room. There was the couch

7

with the long coffee table in front of it and the two chairs wore their summer slip-covers.

"I changed things around a bit," Dad said. "I moved the television set in here because it was cooler."

Dad had stayed alone in the house all summer during the week, except Saturdays and Sundays when he had driven up to Lindsay to be with the boys.

Bruce noticed something new in the room. There was a picture in a silver frame on one of the end tables. It was of Mom, smiling and pretty, and he couldn't bring himself to look at it directly. He gave it a quick glance, then averted his eyes.

Robby had run ahead into the room he shared with Bruce.

"They're all here!" he cried to Bruce. "Jocko, Monko, Wacko and Fido!"

Sometimes Bruce teased his brother for collecting toy stuffed animals. "You're too big for those little things!" he used to sniff. But today he was glad to see the familiar grinning monkeys, the furry kitten and floppy eared dog, all sitting in a row on the toy shelves.

He looked at his own things, the model planes, his stamp album, the large piece of board leaning against the wall to which his train tracks were fastened. Maybe it wasn't so bad—being home.

"Why don't you boys start unpacking this suitcase while I get the rest of the things from the car?" Dad came into the room.

Robby didn't stay very long, and ran off to find Phil Dickerson. Bruce found an old wallet that he thought he had lost in a drawer and there were two dimes in it! He heard Dad bringing things into the house and went to the doorway of his parents' bedroom.

Why was it so different? Then he noticed that Mom's dressing table was swept clean on top, the pretty little bottles that always glittered so brightly were gone. And one of the chests of drawers was missing—

He suddenly felt Dad's hand on his shoulder. "I've changed some things around, son. I'm going to sleep in the study. I put the chest for my clothes in there."

"But who's going to sleep here?" Bruce looked up.

"Don't you remember I told you and Robby that I hired a nice lady to cook and take care of the house?" Dad smiled. "Her name is Mrs. Logan and she'll be here the first thing tomorrow morning. I'm sure you boys will like her. Come on, let me show you how I fixed up the study for myself." Dad drew him away into the other room.

The study was right off the front hall. They used to keep the television set in there so they could watch programs without disturbing Mom and Dad. Now Dad's chest of drawers was in there, but everything else was the same.

"I think I'd better call Grandma and Grandpa," Dad said. "I promised I would as soon as we got home."

While Dad made the phone call Bruce could hear the Dickersons outside. He wondered if they were having company today. They had lots of relatives living nearby while outside of his grandparents Bruce didn't have any other family around here.

Dad seemed to be having quite a long conversation with Grandma so Bruce left the study. He found himself drawn back to the old room that had been Mom's and Dad's.

It was going to seem strange to have someone else living in here. He wondered what Mrs. Logan would be like. He put his hand on the brass knob of a closet and opened it.

Hangers hung neatly in a row without any clothes on them. The shelves and floors were empty, too.

"I gave all of Mom's things away, Bruce." He

whirled about, startled by Dad's voice. "Don't look so frightened, Bruce. It's better to talk about these things. Mom had an old friend, Mrs. Standish, who really needs things and I knew Mom would like her to have some. I took the rest to the Salvation Army. A few things I saved. Grandma is wearing your mother's wrist watch, you know that. Remember the ring with the diamond in it that we always called an engagement ring? I still have that and the pearls I gave Mom once on our anniversary. They're not so valuable but I put them in the bank vault for Robby and you when you're grown up."

Bruce looked bewildered, and Dad laughed.

"I don't mean for you boys to wear!" he went on. "But one day, when Robby and you are young men, you'll meet some nice young ladies, just like I met Mom. You'll want to get married and one of you can give the ring and one of you the pearls to your wives. Don't you think that would be nice, sort of—sort of a present from Mom?"

Bruce gulped and nodded. Before he could say anything the back doorbell rang.

"I'll answer it—" He ran toward the door.

"Hello!" He was pleased to see Jimmy Dickerson there.

12

"My—my mom wants me to ask your dad something," Jimmy said.

"Sure, come on in," Bruce answered.

Jimmy didn't look much different. He had grown bigger but his dark hair hung over his eyes the same way and it was wonderful to see him again.

Jimmy glanced around the living room as if he were finding it strange to be here. Dad had come in and Jimmy began talking in a fast way.

"My mother wants to know if you'd all like to have dinner with us tonight. She says it's nice enough for us to have a barbecue in the back yard. But if you'd all rather be alone why she understands that, too."

"Well, that's awfully nice of her," Dad answered. "I think we'd like to eat with you. We haven't had a barbecue together in a long time. What do you think, Bruce?"

"Oh, yes—" Bruce nodded.

"And—and can't you come out now?" Jimmy asked Bruce. "There's plenty of time to play before we eat."

"Go ahead, Bruce," Dad encouraged him. "I'll finish getting us settled. You haven't seen your old friends in a long time."

Bruce was glad to leave the house. He walked

13

with Jimmy, crossing the driveway that separated his house from the Dickersons'.

"Linda went over to her friend's house," Jimmy said. "She'll be back when we eat."

The Dickerson back yard was always full of things to play with, wagons, bikes, swings—and children. Robby and Phil were there now, just as if they'd never been separated.

"I got this just the other day." Jimmy picked up a football and showed it to Bruce. "Want to kick it around awhile?"

They talked as they played. Bruce told Jimmy about all the swimming and fishing he had done this summer. Jimmy and his family had gone on a camping trip for two weeks, sleeping in tents out of doors.

"I'm glad we're back home now," Jimmy grinned. "And that you're back, too. I was afraid you might move away or something since—since you went to your grandma and grandpa's."

Bruce could tell that Jimmy had almost said "since your mother died." He was glad Jimmy didn't mention that. He didn't like talking about it to anyone.

They were tossing the ball back and forth when a voice broke in. "Hey, can we play with you, too?"

Bruce looked up and saw two boys who were

14

strange to him. One seemed about Jimmy's age and his, with short blond hair and a kind of wise-guy look on his face. The other boy was shorter and younger and was obviously his brother.

"No, you can't play with us," Jimmy retorted, making a forward pass to Bruce. "You're not allowed in this yard, so beat it."

"Aw, come on! You're not still sore about last week, are you?" the bigger boy asked. "I didn't mean to tear your shirt."

"Something always happens when I play with you," Jimmy answered. "My folks said not to play with you, so don't you come into our yard or even on our side of the street."

"I can stay on this side of the street if I want," the boy replied. "You don't own the sidewalk. I've got some money and I was going to treat you but you've a fat chance now! Come on, Stewie!" He yanked the smaller boy along with him.

"Who are they?" Bruce asked Jimmy.

"They moved here during the summer, to the house where the Wilsons used to live, across the street."

"What's the matter with them? You were sure mean to them!" Bruce said.

"They're terrible!" Jimmy answered. "Mom calls

15

them 'the Indians' because they're always getting into trouble. I played with them when they first moved here but something always seemed to happen and now I'm not supposed to play with them any more."

"They didn't seem so awful to me." Bruce shrugged his shoulders.

Late in the afternoon Dad and all the Dickersons came into the back yard.

"My goodness, Bruce, you have grown tall this summer!" Mrs. Dickerson put her arm around him, squeezing him tightly. She was a plump lady, with blonde wavy hair and blue eyes. Bruce had never thought her as pretty as his mother, but somehow you always felt like smiling when you were with her.

Mr. Dickerson brought some old newspapers to start the barbecue fire. He was thin and a bit bald like Dad and they always joked about each other's hair. A few summers ago Mr. Dickerson had helped Dad build the flagstone terrace in back of their house and Dad had helped Mr. Dickerson build the big stone barbecue.

"Hand me some of that kindling and charcoal, will you, boys?" Mr. Dickerson asked as he rolled newspaper for the fire.

16

"Can I light the match to start it?" Bruce asked.

"I want to start it!" Jimmy said.

"No, me!" Phil cried, echoed by Robby's, "No, me!"

"Let's let this girl do it." Mr. Dickerson smiled as Linda came up the walk just then.

Linda was about a year younger than Jimmy and resembled her mother, except that she wasn't plump.

"Gee, I'm glad you're back!" She smiled at Bruce, as she struck the match for the fire.

"I think you'd better all go inside now and wash," Mrs. Dickerson said. "Please don't mess up the bathroom."

It was hard not to mess the bathroom a little, all of them pushing around the sink. Bruce dropped the soap on the floor and they had a terrible scramble for it.

When they came out again hot dogs were sizzling on the grill. Mrs. Dickerson had set a bowl of potato salad on the table, sliced tomatoes and cucumbers, as well as tall glasses of milk.

Everyone talked, laughed and ate at once. The Dickersons told them things that had happened during the summer. Bruce, Robby and Dad told them what they'd done at Grandma and Grandpa's, and

17

also about the new housekeeper coming tomorrow.

"You boys finished? Let me give you your dessert now. I baked an apple pie today." Mrs. Dickerson started to clear the table.

The children helped her, throwing the old paper plates into the barbecue and watching them turn into a banner of fire. Mrs. Dickerson soon brought the pie out. She walked around the table, pouring more milk into the children's glasses. As she stood beside Bruce he looked up at her and suddenly remembered how Mom always loved picnics, either in the back yard or out in the country.

"You serve the pie and I'll take care of the milk!" That was what Mom would say to Mrs. Dickerson if she were here now. He could almost hear her voice.

"Bruce, you're not eating your pie. Don't you like it?" Mrs. Dickerson asked with concern.

"I'm just not hungry any more." He pushed the plate away from him.

"You ought to at least taste it, Bruce," Dad said. "Don't you remember what good pie Mrs. Dickerson always makes?"

"Yes—I remember—" Bruce stood up from his chair. "I—I think I want to go home—" he said. "I—I'm tired—"

18

"Why, of course, run along if you like." Mrs. Dickerson smiled. "You've had a hard day." She started to put her arm around Bruce's shoulder but he pulled away, running toward his house.

Once there the first thing he saw, standing on the table in the living room, was the picture of Mom in the silver frame. He walked over to it, trying to look at it, but he couldn't. Hot tears filled his eyes as he reached out, grabbing the picture by the top of the frame, and thrusting it back on the table, face down.

The tears were running down his cheeks as he flung himself on the bed in his room.

"Mommy—Mommy—" he called, choked with sobs, his hands digging into his pillow.

It wasn't the first time he had cried like this. He had cried and cried right after Mommy died, not believing that she wouldn't come back. He remembered Dad sitting on his bed one night saying, "It's all right to cry, Bruce. We all have a lot of sadness in us, Robby, you and I, Grandpa and Grandma, everyone who knew and loved Mommy. It—it's good to let it out."

He was afraid Dad might come in now, talk to him again. And he didn't feel like talking to anyone. He put on his pajamas quickly, getting into bed just as he heard the back door open.

19

"Bruce—are you all right, Bruce?" he heard Dad calling from inside.

"He's in bed—I think he's sleeping!" Robby was in the room.

"What, already?" He knew Dad was standing beside the bed.

"Why did he run away? Why is he asleep already?" Robby asked.

"I think he wanted to be alone," Dad answered. "Sometimes people just want to be alone. Come on, Robby, you get undressed in the bathroom—"

Bruce felt relieved that Dad was not going to make him talk. He still pretended to be asleep when Robby returned.

"Hop into bed and I'll tuck you in," Dad whispered.

"I'm glad we're home!" Robby said. "I'm going to get up early and play with Phil."

"I'm glad you're home too. I missed having my boys with me all the time," Dad answered. He leaned over, running his hand over Bruce's head, kissing his cheek. "Good night—" he whispered, in such a way that Bruce couldn't tell if Dad knew he was awake or not.

Robby fell asleep right away. Bruce knew from

his breathing. But he lay in bed—his lips suddenly trembling—his eyes filling with tears again. He didn't want to cry like a baby all the time. But he wasn't glad to be home. Because without Mom—it wasn't like home any more.

TWO

"We don't have too much in the house for break-fast," Dad said. "There's orange juice, corn flakes and milk. I think we can manage on that, don't you?"

Bruce and Robby, both in pajamas, were seated at the kitchen table. In cold weather they always had to wear their slippers but it was still quite warm. Their bare toes were curled over the rungs of the chairs. Dad was dressed, ready for work, and looked a little funny with a dish towel tucked in his belt to keep his trousers clean.

"Hey, you've put two spoonfuls of sugar on those corn flakes already," Dad said as Bruce started to dig into the bowl. Just then the doorbell rang. Robby always liked to answer the door and he bounded from his chair.

22

"It must be Mrs. Logan, coming to work for us," Dad said, pulling the towel out of his belt.

Bruce left the table, too, anxious to see what the lady would be like.

"Good morning, Mr. Madison. Did I get here on time? I know you have to get off to work."

"Plenty of time. Let me help you with your cases. Boys, this is Mrs. Logan, whom I've been telling you about. This little fellow is Robby, and the bigger one is Bruce."

"Well, hello! I'm sure we're going to be good friends." Mrs. Logan smiled at them.

Bruce couldn't tell whether he liked her or not. She didn't look too bad, not pretty like Mom, nor as old as Grandma, but sort of in between. She wore a print dress and eyeglasses. Her hair was short and frizzy, all mixed up brown and gray. But it was her feet which surprised both Robby and Bruce. She was wearing sneakers, just like they did!

"This is your room," Dad said. "You'll find plenty of closet space."

"Oh, don't worry about me!" Mrs. Logan's voice was kind of loud. "I'll manage all right."

"Come on, boys, we'll let Mrs. Logan get settled while we finish our breakfast."

"What's she wearing sneakers for?" Bruce asked as they returned to the kitchen.

"Shh—she may hear you," Dad said. "She probably just finds them more comfortable. Don't worry about it. I want you fellows to be sure and cooperate with her. Do whatever she tells you. I've got to get off to work now." Dad drank his coffee.

"Is there anything I can do in here? I can finish getting unpacked later." Mrs. Logan joined them. "My, what a lovely kitchen!"

"The boys are finishing up and they'll get dressed," Dad said. He rose from the table and kissed them both. "I'll give you some money to shop, Mrs. Logan."

Bruce followed his father to the hall. He hated to see Dad leave, to be left with this strange person.

When the door shut he heard Mrs. Logan's voice behind him.

"How about you boys coming back to finish your breakfast?"

"I don't want any more!" Robby said.

"Oh, come now!" Mrs. Logan smiled as she led Robby back into the kitchen. "How do you expect to grow big and tall like your daddy? Come on— both of you!"

24

Bruce didn't feel like eating any more either, but he supposed he'd better finish.

"I have a son," Mrs. Logan said as she looked at the kitchen stove, examined the ice box and cupboards. "He's a big fellow now, married and living in California. But he was once little like you. He ate all his cereal and is he strong!"

Bruce gulped the rest of his breakfast. He decided he'd dress quickly and find Jimmy.

It didn't take him long to put on blue jeans and a tee-shirt. He washed a bit and brushed his teeth with water and no paste.

Mrs. Logan stood in the doorway of the bathroom. "You dropped your towel on the floor, young man!"

Bruce picked it up. "I'm going out—" he said.

"Is this your room?" Mrs. Logan turned to the other doorway. "How about you fellows helping me to tidy it up a bit? Those pajamas and soldiers and books—"

"They're not my pajamas!" Bruce declared.

"The soldiers are yours!" Robby said.

"You were playing with them though!"

"Boys—boys—don't start fighting. I can't stand fighting!" Mrs. Logan exclaimed. "Now come on, each of you pick up your own things. And I want you to pull your sheets and blankets off the bed so they can air in the window."

Mrs. Logan pulled one side of the blankets and sheets and motioned for Bruce to do the other. "I want you to strip your bed like this every morning," she said. "Then take them over to the window like this!"

She opened the window and flung the bedding over the sill. Bruce had seen his mother and grandma do it sometimes but not every day. And he never had to help. If Mrs. Logan thought he was going to do it every day she was crazy but he decided not to get into an argument about it now. He was in a hurry to see Jimmy.

"Hello there!" Bruce was just crossing the driveway to Jimmy's house when he heard the voices from the front sidewalk. He saw the two boys who had moved into the neighborhood during the summer—Frankie and Stewie.

"Hello—" He walked down the driveway toward them. They didn't look like such bad guys to him, he decided. In fact they looked like fun.

"What are you going to do now?" Frankie, the bigger boy, asked, pushing his hair back from his eyes.

"I don't know yet," Bruce answered. "I just came out."

"Have you seen that big hole they dug in the lot on Cambridge Street?" Frankie went on. "They were supposed to build some stores there but they changed their minds. It's fun to play in and we're going down there now. Why don't you come along?"

"Sure, I'd like to. I'll get Jimmy—" Bruce answered.

"We don't need him. Come on—"

Bruce hesitated, not knowing whether to go with them or not. After all, Jimmy was his best friend and he'd hardly seen him. Besides, he remembered that Jimmy didn't want to play with Frankie and Stewie.

"I can't come now. Maybe I'll see you later—" he said, starting for Jimmy's house.

When he knocked at the door, Jimmy, himself, answered.

"I was just getting ready to come see you. Wait a sec—" Jimmy lifted his foot to a chair and tied a loose shoelace. "Want to take a bike ride this morning?"

"All right!" Bruce agreed. "Gee—I wonder if Dad took them to work with him. They were tied on the car—"

But both his bike and Robby's were in the garage,

leaning against the wall as if they were glad to be back where they belonged.

Soon the boys were riding down the street, side by side.

"Did the new lady come to work for you this morning?" Jimmy asked.

"Yeah, she did." Bruce nodded.

"Is she nice?"

"I don't know yet. She seemed a little bit bossy. She made me take all the bedding off my bed and put it in the window."

"Oh, I do that for my mother sometimes," Jimmy said.

"But she wants me to do it every day! Say—I saw those new fellows, Frankie and Stewie, just before I came to your house. They said there's a big hole dug on Cambridge Street. Where they were supposed to build stores. Want to go there?"

"Not if they're going to be there!"

"They don't seem so terrible to me," Bruce said.

"They are though. I told you, I always get into trouble when I play with them." Jimmy was insistent.

29

"Why are they like that?" Bruce asked.

"Mom says it's because both their mother and father work all day and just let Frankie and Stewie shift for themselves. Mom says it's almost as bad as if they didn't have a mother—" and then Jimmy stopped short, realizing what he had said.

Bruce realized it, too. His cheeks turned crimson and he felt a terrible, sinking feeling inside of him. But he didn't want Jimmy to know it.

"I'll race you to the corner!" he said, dashing ahead on his bike.

He tried not to think of what Jimmy had said for the rest of the morning, but he couldn't forget it. They rode as far as Clayton Park, rested on the grass, watched some fellows playing ball, and then rode back home again.

"Want to come to my house for lunch?" Jimmy asked. "It'll be all right with my mother."

"No—thanks." Bruce didn't feel like seeing Mrs. Dickerson. "I'd better go in. Mrs. Logan will be expecting me."

He was hot and thirsty as he entered the house.

"Hello, that you, Bruce?" he heard Mrs. Logan call from Dad's room.

"Yep!" He went straight to the ice box and took

out a bottle of milk. He found a glass in the cup-
board and started to pour the milk.

"I wondered if you'd be along soon." Mrs. Logan
came into the kitchen. "Robby isn't here yet. Bruce,
be careful, you're spilling milk."

He saw some drops on the linoleum. "Oh, I'm
sorry," he said, and started to rub his sneaker over
them.

"Let me wipe it up. That only makes it worse!"
Mrs. Logan took a mop out of the closet and cleaned
the spot. "Have you always been allowed to go to
the ice box and help yourself to whatever you want,
Bruce?" she asked.

"Oh, sure!" he answered. "What are we having
for lunch?"

"I made a surprise for you boys. I hope you like
it. Bruce, I don't think you ought to drink any more
milk before eating. You'll spoil your appetite—"

"Well—all right—" He reluctantly put the bottle
of milk back, even though he was still thirsty.

"Go wash your hands and I'll have your lunch set
out for you when you come back."

He shuffled off to the bathroom. He wasn't going
to like Mrs. Logan. She acted so bossy about everything. He was glad to be alone in the bathroom.

"Let me in! I wanta wash, too!" He heard Robby pounding at the bathroom door.

"All right—all right!" He dried his hands and opened the door.

He had to admit, though, that lunch was good. There were egg salad sandwiches that were really delicious, and carrots cut into sticks, and cup cakes with chocolate frosting.

"Have all the cakes you want." Mrs. Logan smiled as she saw the boys' looks of approval. "I baked them this morning. That's one thing I love to do— bake cakes and cookies."

"Can you make chocolate brownies?" Bruce asked.

"Oh, yes, I'll make them one day this week."

Maybe she wasn't so bad, after all, Bruce decided as he ate a third cup cake. Just then he felt Robby's foot kicking against his leg.

"Stop kicking!" he said and gave him a poke back with his foot.

"I didn't kick you!" Robby exclaimed indignantly.

"You did, too! There—you just did it again!"

"Oh, I was just swinging my leg—"

"Boys, don't squabble!" Mrs. Logan came to the table. "If there's one thing I can't stand, that's two boys quarreling. I told your father when he spoke to me about this job that I'm not used to children any more. I'm sure we'll get along all right though, if you will just try to behave—"

"I'm going out!" Bruce said, wiping the crumbs off his mouth with the back of his hand.

"Bruce—you ought to wash your hands—" He heard Mrs. Logan's voice trailing after him to the door, but he pretended that he didn't.

He began to walk toward Jimmy's house but then he remembered their bike ride and what Jimmy had said about the boys across the way. *It's almost as bad as if they didn't have any mother—*

Maybe he'd skip playing with Jimmy this afternoon. He had some money in his pocket that Grandpa had given him. He hadn't been down to the corner store yet.

As he walked along the street, the sound of water from a hose came to him. He looked up and saw Frankie and Stewie. They were watering their front lawn and looked as if they were having a good time doing it.

"It's my turn now! Let me do it awhile!" Stewie was shouting to Frankie.

Why shouldn't he go over and talk to them? Bruce wondered. Maybe Jimmy didn't like them but he didn't know everything. Mrs. Logan probably wouldn't like them either, but she wasn't his boss. She wasn't his mother. He didn't have to do everything she told him. And after all, Frankie and Stewie didn't have a mother around during the day either. They'd probably all get along very well together.

He thrust his hands into the pockets of his jeans and sauntered across the street.

"Hi, fellows!" he called as he came near them. "What are you doing?"

THREE

"Hello! We're watering the lawn—" Frankie seemed surprised that Bruce had come over. But he also seemed pleased.

"Come on, give me a turn!" Stewie was still trying to get the hose from his brother. In their struggle over it the spray of water hit the side of the house.

"The house sure is dusty from the summer. Let's wash it clean," Frankie said.

Bruce watched them as they ran the hose from side to side along the white clapboards. Streaks of dirty water ran down and he wasn't convinced that the house would look better. But it did look like fun.

"Want a turn?" Frankie held the hose out to Bruce, careful not to point the water at him.

"Oh—yes!" Bruce exclaimed.

He gripped the hose. Water trickled from the nozzle and he tried not to get it on his jeans or sneakers. It was fun playing the water on the house, though he knew that he wouldn't dare do a thing like this at his own place.

"We had a swell time at the big hole this morning!" Frankie said. "Want to go there now?"

Bruce hesitated, but not for long. If he were going to play with Frankie and Stewie, be their friend, why shouldn't he go to the lots?

"All right! I'll go!" he answered.

Stewie turned off the water, Frankie took the hose from Bruce and dropped it on the lawn. Bruce knew that his father always insisted the hose be rolled up and put away but some people did leave theirs out all the time.

"Let's get some guns to take along!" Frankie said. "Come on in the house with us."

Bruce followed them through the back door. It was a nice house, with a pretty kitchen, but there were still the remains of breakfast all over, dirty dishes and glasses, ashtrays filled with cigarette butts, and even a piece of toast on the floor.

The boys led him into the bedroom, which looked just as disorderly.

"Here's a good gun for you!" Frankie tossed Bruce a long toy rifle, while he fastened a leather holster around his own waist. He gripped the two

36

bone-handled, gleaming pistols that protruded from the holsters. Stewie found a short, pearl gun and then they all ran out of the house.

"To the lots! To the Grand Canyon!" Frankie called, running with a gallop down the street. Stewie and Bruce hurried after him, echoing his words, "To the lots! To the Grand Canyon!"

Cambridge Street was about four blocks away and the hole was big and impressive. The boys slid down the side, a good deal of loose dirt attaching itself to them.

"Bang! Bang! There's an Indian hiding behind that ambush!" Frankie cried. "You be an Indian!" He pointed his guns at Stewie. "Fall down dead!"

"I'm an Indian! But I'm not going to be dead. I'm going to scalp you!"

Stewie leapt at Frankie in a fierce way that frightened Bruce for the first moment, but then turned out to be exciting. The two boys grappled, turning and struggling in the dust.

"Bang! Bang!" Bruce turned his rifle on them. "I've shot both of you dead!"

"Just a shoulder wound." Frankie's face twisted with make-believe pain as he gripped his shoulder. "But I'm Sure-Shot Lefty. I can shoot you with my left hand. Bang! Bang!"

"I'll get him, too!" Stewie leapt at Bruce the way he had at Frankie. Now Bruce and he rolled in the dirt. Bruce's mouth felt gritty as some dirt got into it. But Stewie was smaller and he soon had him pinned to the ground.

"Be a wrestler!" Frankie cried to Bruce. "Twist his arm! Make him say 'uncle'!"

"No, I don't want to do that!" Bruce said, getting off Stewie. He glanced at his clothes, grinned. "Gosh, are we dirty!"

"Let's go back to the house and wash up under the hose," Frankie suggested.

Bang! Bang! They pretended they were the Sheriff's posse after Jesse James, all the way back home. Stewie was turning on the hose when Frankie said, "Let's get into our bathing suits. It's warm enough."

Bruce glanced toward his house warily. He had a feeling that Mrs. Logan wouldn't like him to get into a bathing suit.

"I—I think mine is packed away already," he said to the boys. "We didn't think we'd go swimming any more this summer."

"We'll lend you one. We've got an extra one," Frankie said.

Three piles of clothes added to the litter on the bedroom floor. Bruce managed to twist into the bathing suit Frankie gave him and then they hurried out to the lawn.

Stewie turned on the water and Frankie grabbed the hose. He made a high arc of water and then brought it lower. "Go on—I'll spray you," he said to Bruce.

Stewie ran through the water first, screaming, "It's cold—it's cold!"

Bruce ran through it next. He didn't think it was so terribly cold and he rubbed some of the dirt off.

"Want me to hold it for you?" he asked Frankie.

"Let me make the spray finer." Frankie turned the nozzle. "Oh, look!" he exclaimed. "Here comes Nancy Adamson. Let's scare her."

Bruce had known Nancy for a long time. She lived around the block and right now she looked as if she were returning from her piano lesson. She had some rolled up music under her arm, and was dressed up. Many children in the neighborhood took lessons from Mrs. Painter who had a sign, "MUSIC INSTRUCTION," on her front lawn.

"Hello, Nancy! How are you, Nancy?" Frankie had turned the hose nozzle to a long, steady stream again. He held the hose so that a curve of water went into the air and came to the ground just behind Nancy.

"Don't you get me wet!" Nancy's eyes blazed at Frankie.

"Well, walk a little faster then. We want to wash the sidewalk." Frankie kept the water dripping close to Nancy's heels even though she did walk faster.

"Hey, you'd better be careful," Bruce said. "You'll really get her wet."

"Oh, a little water won't hurt her. She ain't sugar, she won't melt. Watch her walk faster. Look out, Nancy—" Frankie ran with the hose to keep up with her.

It was kind of funny, the way Nancy increased her pace—only a little, because she didn't want to show that she could be bossed by a bunch of boys.

"Faster, Nancy—hurry up, Nancy—" Frankie ran down the walk after her, pulling the hose with him.

Stewie was doubled up with laughter, and Bruce couldn't help grinning widely. But suddenly Nancy let out a shriek.

"O—ow! Look what you've done to me! O—ow— I'm soaking wet!"

It had happened! Bruce didn't know whether Frankie had done it deliberately or not—but Nancy was soaking wet! She ran down the street toward her house, holding her limp sheet music, her clothes and hair dripping. Her voice rang through the air.

"You did it on purpose! I'm going to tell my mother—on all of you!"

"Oh, boy! We'd better put the hose away and beat it!" Frankie said. "Turn it off, Stewie!"

Stewie turned it off and they went inside to dress. "What'll we do now?" Frankie asked. "Want to go to the corner store and get a soda?"

"No, I don't think so," Bruce replied. "It's getting near dinner time and my dad will be home soon." He glanced around the boys' kitchen. "Doesn't your mother come home to make dinner soon?"

"Not until sometime after six. I'm hungry. Come on, let's go to the store, Stewie."

"I'll see you guys again," Bruce called as he walked across the street to his house.

He glanced toward the Dickersons but none of them were in sight. He'd had lots of fun with Frankie and Stewie this afternoon. Jimmy was crazy not to like them.

A warm, wonderful smell reached Bruce's nose as he entered the house. Chocolate! He followed it to the kitchen and saw Mrs. Logan cutting up brownies in a pan and arranging them on a plate.

"You said you liked them!" She smiled at him so that he almost liked her. "Robby's in the bathroom washing up and changing his shirt. You run along and do that too."

Later, when Robby and he were in the living room, looking at TV, Bruce suddenly noticed that the picture in the silver frame—the picture of Mom —was no longer in the room. Had Mrs. Logan moved it? What had she done with it?

"Did you see the picture—the one in the silver frame?" He went into the dining alcove where Mrs. Logan was setting the table.

"The one of your mother?" Mrs. Logan asked. "I saw it in your father's room when I straightened up in there. Isn't that where it's always kept?"

"I—I guess so—" Bruce answered. His face suddenly felt hot. Dad must have moved the picture— after finding it turned down—the way it had been left last night. Well—he'd rather have it in Dad's room than in here.

"That's Dad—I heard the car!" Robby scrambled to his feet, and hurried to the back door.

"Hello, how are my fine fellows this evening?" Bruce was happy to see his father.

"Dinner's ready whenever you are," Mrs. Logan said.

At the table Bruce noticed that Dad sat where Mom used to, and Mrs. Logan in Dad's old place.

Dinner was good, tomato juice, meat loaf, mashed potatoes, peas and salad as well as the brownies with peaches.

"I just made a simple meal for this first day," Mrs. Logan said.

"It's delicious," Dad answered. "Come on, Robby, show Mrs. Logan how much you like it."

Robby often fussed at meals and this was going to be one of those evenings, Bruce could see that. He'd hardly touched his meat, and he was picking up his mashed potatoes with his fingers.

"I don't like the meat," Robby complained. "I don't want my salad, either."

"Robby, if you don't eat, you won't be able to look at TV after dinner," Dad said.

"I once read an article that said if children don't eat you should just take the food away from them," Mrs. Logan put in.

Dad seemed a bit annoyed at Mrs. Logan's suggestion. Bruce decided that maybe Dad didn't think Mrs. Logan was so wonderful. But the brownies were pretty good, he had to admit.

"What did you do all day, Bruce?" Dad turned to him from Robby.

"Oh—I played in a big hole on Cambridge Street."

"Didn't you think it was a bit cold to be under

44

that hose?" Mrs. Logan asked as she cleared some dishes from the table.

Bruce gave her a sharp glance. What had she been doing, spying on him?

"It is rather late in the season to get under the hose," Dad said.

"Aw, it was all right!" Bruce grumbled. "I played with those new boys across the street. They're fun."

"I've heard about them," Dad said. "Mrs. Dickerson was telling me that she's had to keep them off the property—"

"I like them!" Bruce said defiantly. "They're as good as Jimmy or any of the Dickerson kids!"

"Well—as long as you're careful and don't get into any real trouble with them. And next time before you go under a hose or do anything like that, you ask Mrs. Logan for permission."

What did Dad think he was anyway, a baby, having to ask Mrs. Logan for permission to do every little thing? He went into his room in an angry mood, and then decided to work on a model plane he hadn't quite finished before the summer began. He was busy with it when the front doorbell rang. He started to go into the living room, curious to know who it was, and then he recognized the voice!

It was Mrs. Adamson—Nancy Adamson's mother!

She was talking to Dad and suddenly Dad's voice rang out.

"Bruce, will you come here a minute?"

He could feel his heart beating faster as he entered the living room. Nancy must have told her mother about Frankie, Stewie and him! He stood quite a distance from them, seeing Mrs. Adamson with Dad, and Mrs. Logan in the doorway of the dining alcove.

"Bruce, did anything happen while you were playing with the boys across the street?" Dad asked him.

"Why—why, we were just having fun—" Bruce stammered, though he knew what this was going to lead to.

"Nancy didn't say it was entirely Bruce's fault," Mrs. Adamson put in. "But that he was with those boys, laughing and encouraging them to spray her."

"I didn't wet her!" Bruce declared.

"Nancy had on one of her best dresses," Mrs. Adamson continued. "It isn't exactly fun to get soaking wet. I don't think you ought to let Bruce play with those boys. They're up to mischief every minute of the day. There hasn't been any peace in the neighborhood since they moved here."

"Well, I don't think they should have sprayed

Nancy," Dad said. "But boys that age are bound to get into trouble now and then. And I don't like to tell Bruce with whom he should play and with whom he shouldn't. I think children should be allowed to choose their own friends. However, I'm sure Bruce is sorry he had any part in getting Nancy wet. Aren't you, Bruce?"

Bruce felt relieved that Dad didn't sound any madder. "Yes—I'm sorry—" he said.

"Well, just see that it doesn't happen again," Mrs. Adamson declared. "And mark my word, Mr. Madison, you'll be sorry if you let your boys play with those young scamps."

After Mrs. Adamson left Dad turned to Bruce. "I meant what I said. I think you should choose your own friends, Bruce, but you'll have to watch your step and keep from getting in trouble. Now get back to whatever you were doing. I brought some work from the office that I have to get done."

Bruce saw Mrs. Logan going back to the kitchen, shaking her head on the way—as if she thought that Dad had let him off too easily. Well, let her think what she wanted to. Dad was his boss—not Mrs. Logan!

FOUR

As the days went by Bruce grew more and more accustomed to being at home again, but the house still seemed strange without Mom. Coming home from play and finding Mrs. Logan there wasn't the same as having a mother, even on days when she wasn't so bad.

The best thing about Mrs. Logan was that she liked to bake and there were always plenty of cakes and cookies in the kitchen. But she was still a bit too strict about the boys keeping the place in order and whenever they scrapped, even in fun, she would exclaim, "You must stop it! I can't stand fighting! It makes me nervous!"

That was the main trouble with Mrs. Logan, Bruce once heard Dad tell someone on the phone. Although she was a nice person, too many little, unimportant things bothered her.

Robby seemed to get along in their new way of living better than Bruce. Sometimes it seemed to Bruce that his brother didn't miss Mom at all! He was always busy, playing with Phil next door, running over to the Dickersons' right after breakfast, staying until lunch time, coming home for a bite to eat, and hurrying back there again.

"I hardly ever see him!" Mrs. Logan complained to Dad. "Maybe you ought to speak to Mrs. Dickerson about it. If she sent Robby home instead of keeping him there so much, I could spend more time with him."

"Robby has known Mrs. Dickerson from the time he was a baby," Dad said. "I think it does him good to be there right now, so let's not worry about it."

Even though Frankie and Stewie had gotten Bruce in trouble he was still friendly with them, though he played mostly with Jimmy. After all, Jimmy and he had known each other almost all their lives. They had had many disagreements so even if they didn't feel the same way about Frankie and Stewie they could go on being friends. Jimmy played with other boys at times, also, which gave Bruce a chance to see Frankie and Stewie.

The weather began to get cooler and school was scheduled to start again. Bruce found himself wondering who his teacher would be. He was even a bit eager to go to school, although he had been glad to start vacation the end of last term.

Jimmy and he set out together the first morning of school, Robby and Phil walking ahead of them. Jimmy's sister, Linda, had gone earlier to pick up a girl friend.

"I'm glad we're going to be in the same room," Jimmy said.

They were both entering the fifth grade. Last term they had been in the same classroom but the year before they hadn't.

"Look, they've painted the fence!" Bruce exclaimed as they approached the school yard. The fence gleamed with a coat of bright aluminum paint.

Boys and girls were streaming into the yard, greeting each other with smiles, talk, and even affectionate punches. When the bell rang they all went into the school.

"Hello, Bruce! I'm glad to see you back again!" He was startled to be addressed by Mr. Rogers, the principal. Not only was he being addressed, but Mr. Rogers was standing in front of him, stopping to have a personal chat.

"I heard you spent the summer with your grandparents." Mr. Rogers smiled at him. "I met your dad downtown one day and he told me. Bruce, if anything comes up this term that bothers you, don't hesitate to come into my office and talk to me. At any time, do you understand that?"

"Yes, sir, I do." Bruce nodded.

Jimmy had gone ahead and Bruce walked down the rest of the hall to his classroom.

He knew why Mr. Rogers had stopped and talked to him that way. It was because of Mom. Mr. Rogers meant to be nice because he felt sorry for Bruce since his mother had died. Bruce knew that, even though Mr. Rogers hadn't mentioned his mother.

As he came into his classroom, he saw lots of familiar faces from last term. Everyone smiled at him but at the same time he saw an expression on each face that disturbed him.

Everyone was glad to see him but he could tell what each person was thinking. *"Bruce doesn't have a mother any more!"*

"Hello, Bruce! Why don't you take that seat there." Even Miss Hayden, the teacher, spoke to him in a special sort of way. He didn't want the seat she motioned for him to take. It was way up front. He walked to the back of the room and to his delight he saw Frankie sitting there, grinning at him.

"Hi!" he whispered to Frankie and sank into a seat next to him.

However, when permanent seats were assigned for the term, he didn't sit next to either Frankie or Jimmy.

After school hours he played sometimes with Jimmy, other days with Frankie and Stewie. There was something exciting about the way those brothers played, and they managed to stay out of trouble for the time being.

The day of the week that Bruce enjoyed the most was Sunday. In the first place Mrs. Logan left the house early, to be gone all day. Bruce liked being home alone with just Robby and Dad.

Mrs. Logan would leave breakfast for them in the kitchen because Dad usually slept late on Sunday morning. Bruce and Robby played around the house by themselves, looking at the comics or watching TV, with one ear tuned to Dad's room, hoping he would wake up.

"Why do you have to sleep so late?" Bruce asked Dad one Sunday. The minute they heard their father stirring they both hopped into bed with him.

"Because I didn't go to bed until late last night," Dad said. "The party at the Wilsons' house didn't end until after two o'clock."

"Why do you go out every Saturday night?" Bruce asked. "And on some other nights during the week, too? We like it better when you stay home."

Dad tousled Bruce's hair. "I know you do, fellows. But to tell you the truth, I get lonesome staying home by myself. There isn't anybody for me to talk to—"

"There's Mrs. Logan!" Robby protested.

"Well—yes—Mrs. Logan is here. And she's a nice person. But—well, she's a friend of ours but not in the same way my other friends are. Also—" Bruce noticed that Dad hesitated a moment. "Well, also the Wilsons had a lady at their house they wanted me to meet. Her husband died a long time ago and I guess the Wilsons think it would be nice if I married her."

"Married her!" Bruce looked alarmed. "Are you going to marry her?"

"No!" Dad laughed. "Don't look so worried. She was nice but I don't intend to marry for a long time yet. Still, I will take people out once in a while, Bruce and Robby. To restaurants for dinner, and to movies and to visit friends. And someday I might meet someone whom we all will like, and I might marry her. Then you'll have a new mother and I'll have a wife. That—that's a better way to live than the way we do now. And Mom would want things to be that way, too."

Bruce was quiet. He supposed a nice lady, who was a mother, would be better than Mrs. Logan. But he didn't want another lady for a mother—he still wanted—Mom back—

He felt Dad's hand tighten on his arm. "But we're a nice little family by ourselves now, Robby, you, and me, don't you think? And I'll tell you what. Instead of eating the cold cereal Mrs. Logan usually leaves us, how would it be if we all pitched in and tried our hand at something fancier—like, say, an omelet?"

Bruce broke the eggs in the bowl, Robby added the milk. Dad got the frying pan hot. Soon they were sitting at the table, eating the delicious golden omelet with jelly and toast.

"Well, what shall we fellows do today?" Dad asked as he sipped his second cup of coffee.

"Let's go to the movies!" Robby exclaimed. "We haven't been to the movies for a long time!"

"A long time! We went the Sunday before last!" Dad said.

"Could we drive to Grandma's?" Bruce asked.

"Oh, no, that's too far to go and come back in one day. And Grandpa and Grandma wrote that

54

they'd be down to see us before too long. How'd you like to drive out to the Stantons'? You remember Scotty and Lita, don't you? I met them downtown the other day. They said for us to phone and come out any Sunday we feel like it."

Bruce remembered Lita and Scotty Stanton well. He had fun there even though the Stantons didn't have any children. They lived out of town, in a big old house with a wonderful red barn.

Dad phoned them and they said they'd be delighted to have company. The boys didn't have to get all dressed up because they would be climbing trees and running around.

It was nice driving out in the car. All three of them sat up in front, the way they had when they came home from Grandma and Grandpa's. Bruce remembered that before Mom died, they hadn't been able to all sit in the front. Then he pushed that thought away. It seemed wrong to think of anything being better now!

The leaves were turning on the trees, some falling and blowing across the road, like red, brown and gold butterflies chasing each other. The air was a bit nippy, too.

"Just cool enough to make you feel good!" Dad

said, taking a deep breath. Bruce and Robby imitated him, taking deep breaths, too.

They came to the small town where the Stantons lived. The house was at the end of a dirt road, a low white place with black shutters. The Stantons' Irish setter, Lucky, barked as they pulled up. "Quiet, Lucky!" Lita and Scotty came out onto the side porch.

Bruce felt glad to see these old friends. Lita and Scotty, both in slacks and sweaters, greeted them warmly. They didn't say, "My, you've grown!" the way most people did. Instead Scotty grinned. "You guys know the way to the barn, don't you? I suppose you want to go there."

"Beat you to it!" Bruce said to Robby. Of course it was easy to beat his brother and he pushed open the barn door.

Once the place had been used for cows and horses

but now the stalls were empty. Scotty had a work
bench and power saw in one corner but the boys
knew better than to touch any of the tools. There
was a ladder to a loft and on the floor below a stack
of hay. Lita and Scotty had a fresh load of hay put
in every season just for young visitors to jump on.

Bruce and Robby climbed to the loft, jumped
down to the pile of hay, laughing and rolling in it.
When they grew tired of this, they played in an
old wagon which the Stantons had once bought at
an auction sale. It was fun to say, "Gidyap, gidyap,
Trigger!" as if they were riding across the plains.

57

They finally grew tired of the barn and returned to the house.

"We're having a drink. You boys are in time for a coke or ginger ale." Lita greeted them with a smile. "And this is a neighbor of ours who dropped in, Mrs. Gorman. Helen, this is Bruce and Robby Madison."

"My boys!" Dad beamed, flicking a piece of hay out of Robby's hair.

"Mrs. Gorman lives just up the road," Lita explained. "Or rather she did until now but she's just sold her house and is moving into town. There was a big sale at her place yesterday. You sold just about everything, didn't you, Helen?"

"Almost everything!" Mrs. Gorman smiled. She was very pretty with short, fluffy blonde hair and a bright smile. "I have some dishes left, and the people who were supposed to buy that old camp trailer of mine changed their minds. I suppose I'll end up by having to have it hauled away."

"A camp trailer? What's that?" Robby asked.

"Oh, it's not the big kind of house trailer that people live in," Mrs. Gorman explained. "It's more like a wooden platform on wheels, with a tent attached to the top. My husband and I used to go on

58

camping trips. We'd carry our supplies and sleep in it at night."

"Gee, it sounds wonderful!" Bruce exclaimed.

"It is. I wonder—" Mrs. Gorman looked at Dad. "Would you like the boys to have it? Not for camping, but it would be fun to use as a tent or clubhouse if you have room in your back yard."

"Oh, could we have it, Dad? Could we have it?" Bruce's voice was pleading.

"I don't know." Mr. Madison looked a bit doubtful. "It would depend on how big it is."

"Why don't we all walk over and take a look at it now," Scotty suggested.

Everyone agreed to that. Bruce and Robby ran up the road ahead of the others.

"That's the house!" Mrs. Gorman called as they came to a small house painted red like a barn. "I hated selling the place. But I've been living out here alone since my husband died a few years ago and I think I'd enjoy myself more now in the city."

Bruce knew he had to have the trailer the moment he saw it. It was just as Mrs. Gorman had described it, only more wonderful, a wooden platform with a tent on top, perched on what looked like automobile wheels. He scrambled into it, followed by Robby.

"Look, it has a bench all around." Robby sat down.

"That's a place to store things." Bruce lifted the top of one of the benches. It was warm and snug inside the trailer, too, though one of the side flaps of the tent was open to let in air.

"All the sides can be lifted up," Mrs. Gorman explained. "Do you really want the boys to have it?" she asked Dad who was peering into the trailer, too.

"How can I say no?" Dad laughed. "But we'll take it only on one condition. That you sell it to us—"

"Oh, no! I'm glad to have it taken away and to know the boys will enjoy it."

"How'll we get it home?" Bruce thrust his head out to talk to the adults.

"The bumper on Helen's car is equipped to pull

it," Scotty said. "She'll have to pull it into town for you."

"But when will we get it?" Robby asked with concern.

"I'll pull it in with you, when you're ready to go home today," Mrs. Gorman promised.

They had a good dinner at the Stantons' later. Bruce and Robby ate fast so they could start for home, but the grown ups spent a lot of time talking over their coffee. Finally, however, they were ready to leave.

Mrs. Gorman pulled her car out of the garage, backing it up to the trailer. Scotty hitched it to the car. Mrs. Gorman moved forward then. The trailer followed along—ready to go to Bruce's house!

"Why don't I ride with Mrs. Gorman and show her the way?" Bruce suggested, anxious that she shouldn't get lost.

"That's a fine idea," Dad said. "Robby and I will ride together ahead of you."

They said good-bye to Scotty and Lita, and then Bruce got in beside Mrs. Gorman in her car.

It was still light out, and Bruce was proud of the way people in other cars turned to look at the trailer. Mrs. Gorman was easy to talk to and she told him about different camping trips she had taken with the trailer.

"The next turn is our street! See, where Dad is going!" Bruce sat on the edge of his seat.

Dad pulled to the front of the house, motioning for Mrs. Gorman to go up the driveway.

"You'll have to drive right over the grass into the yard," Dad said. He directed Mrs. Gorman, finally telling her when to stop. Then Bruce and she got out of the car and watched Dad unhitch the trailer.

"It's all yours now!" Mrs. Gorman smiled at Bruce and Robby after she pulled her car to the front of the house.

"Won't you come in a little while before you start back?" Dad asked Mrs. Gorman.

"I'm going to stay out in the trailer!" Bruce cried.

"Me, too!" Robby tagged after him.

It was the coziest, most wonderful place in the world, Bruce thought as he sat inside it. He could hardly wait to show it to all the kids, Jimmy, Linda, Frankie, Stewie—

"Boys! Mrs. Gorman is leaving now!" Dad called after a while.

They scrambled out to say good-bye. "Gee—I don't know how to thank you for the trailer!" Bruce beamed, not needing any prompting to be polite.

"Just enjoy yourself in it!" Mrs. Gorman said.

"It's time to turn in now, fellows. I let you stay up late tonight," Dad said as Mrs. Gorman drove away.

"Gosh, what a day!" Bruce exclaimed, taking a last look at the trailer through the window before he went to bed.

The sun and Bruce were up at practically the same time the next morning. He got into his clothes quickly and tiptoed through the living room to the back door. He ran across the yard, into the trailer.

It was a trailer and at the same time it was Fort Apache being attacked by the Indians! It was a police car chasing bandits. It was a jet plane soaring high over the clouds and it was a rocket ship going straight to the moon. It was a wonderful place to be in by himself.

"Bruce, Bruce, breakfast is ready and Mrs. Logan wants you right away!" He could hear Robby calling.

He hated to leave the trailer but he did. Never had he eaten breakfast as quickly, so that he could hurry back to the trailer before it was time to go to school.

It was hard to pay attention in class that day. As

soon as school let out Bruce scurried across the playground, straight to his back yard.

"Gosh, where did you get it! It's terrific!" Jimmy exclaimed later when he saw the trailer. Frankie and Stewie came over to comment on it, too.

Bruce let them all in and for once they were friends together. Later Robby brought Phil over, and Linda came with some of her girl friends. Even Mrs. Dickerson peered in with Taffy.

When Mrs. Logan called the boys in to wash for dinner that evening, Bruce hated to leave the trailer. He wished he could eat his dinner in it.

"Eat your dinner in it! Where did you ever get such an idea?" Mrs. Logan exclaimed. "In fact I think that trailer spoils the back yard. It used to be so pretty."

It was during dinner, with Dad at home, that Bruce got what he considered an even better idea than eating in the trailer.

"Could I sleep in it tonight?" he asked Dad. "It's not very cold out. I could take the mattress from my bed and plenty of blankets."

Bruce held his breath while Dad considered. "Well, I don't suppose it would hurt you."

"I want to sleep in it too!" Robby chimed in.

"No, I want to do it all alone!" Bruce exclaimed. He didn't know why but somehow it seemed important to sleep in it alone this first time.

"All right, I'll let you do it," Dad said, even though Mrs. Logan looked as if she disapproved. "But if you get cold, or even a bit scared, you won't hesitate to come back into the house, will you, Bruce?"

"No, I won't. Gee, Dad, thanks!" Bruce hugged his father.

Dad helped him carry his mattress through the back door to the trailer. It fit almost as if it had been made for the trailer floor. Together Dad and Bruce put the sheets on, then plenty of blankets.

"It looks like fun. Maybe I'll try it some night." Dad grinned.

Usually Bruce had to be coaxed to go to bed but tonight he could hardly wait until it was time to go to sleep. It was decided that he would get into his pajamas, robe and slippers in the house and then dash out to the trailer. He was ready for bed even before Robby.

"I'll tuck you in." Dad smiled, following him through the yard.

It was just getting dark and Bruce took off his robe and slippers, putting them on one of the side benches. Then he crept into bed, pulling the blankets up.

"Guess I can't reach you way up there. I'll just have to tuck your toes in." Dad laughed as he leaned through the open flap and smoothed the blankets. "Good night, son, and remember, if you change your mind the back door will be unlocked."

"Good night, Dad—" Bruce folded his hands behind his head and lay there peacefully.

Through the open flap he could see the stars twinkling in the sky. He wondered if the moon was out. He couldn't see it from here. He snuggled deeper under the blankets as a cool wind blew over him. From somewhere he heard music playing, soft, gentle music. This was his house—his very own—without Mrs. Logan or anybody to tell him what to do. He was out here alone—and nobody could see him except—maybe—Mom—

He bit his lip knowing that tears were filling his eyes, knowing also why he liked this trailer so much —why he wanted to be in it alone like this.

The house over there, where he had always lived, wasn't like home any more. Mom wasn't there—the way she used to be. Everything was different in there—while out here—this was a new house with room just for him—and for thinking about Mom.

He closed his eyes and he could remember the way his mother used to lean over and tuck the satin binding of the blanket under his chin.

"Good night, Bruce boy. Sleep well with a happy dream!"

FIVE

One weekend Grandma and Grandpa drove down for a visit. They had written that they were coming and Bruce looked forward to it for days ahead of time.

Mrs. Logan cleaned the house thoroughly for the visit. Bruce had to spend more than an hour straightening his room. Somehow he didn't mind this time, and Robby pitched in, too.

Grandma and Grandpa arrived on Saturday morning, to stay until Sunday afternoon. Mrs. Logan was going to sleep at a friend's house for the weekend, so Grandpa and Grandma could have her room.

"They're here! They're here!" Robby was the first to see the car pull up at about eleven o'clock Saturday morning. Bruce hadn't even gone near his trailer today, he was so anxious to see his grandparents.

There were hugs and kisses and exclamations about how well everyone looked. Dad introduced Mrs. Logan to Grandma and Grandpa and there were presents for the boys, stamps for Bruce's album and a stuffed elephant with real ivory tusks for Robby. Grandma also brought a box of cookies and Bruce didn't think that Mrs. Logan seemed too pleased about that, though she tasted one and said, "My, they're delicious. You must give me the recipe."

Mrs. Logan left right after lunch. The house seemed so different with Grandma and Grandpa here, Bruce thought. He listened to all the news of things that had happened in the country since summer and then they told Grandma and Grandpa about things here.

Bruce hung around the kitchen while Grandma made dinner.

"Well, it looks as if Mrs. Logan takes good care of you," Grandma said.

"Oh, I don't like her much," Bruce answered.

"No? Why not? She seems very nice—"

"She's okay in some ways. But she's too fussy. I can't even take a glass of milk or anything out of the ice box when I feel like it. And if Robby and I fool

69

around just a little bit she says it makes her nervous!"

"Sometimes your fooling around used to make
me nervous, too!" Grandma smiled. "Why don't you
help yourself to a glass of milk now? Dinner won't
be ready for quite a while."

This was one night when Bruce didn't think about
sleeping in the trailer either. He was happy in his
own bed, hearing the murmur of the grown ups'
voices inside.

Sunday went by all too fast, even though they
didn't do much, and at four o'clock Grandma and
Grandpa decided that they had better start for
home. Bruce hated to see the car pull away, with
Grandpa and Grandma in it waving good-bye to
them. The house seemed empty when Dad, Robby
and he returned to it.

When he awakened the next morning he felt terribly cranky. Mrs. Logan said something to him
about being sure to air his bedding.

"I don't feel like it!" he said and ran off to school.

He felt that way all week long, and spent all the
spare time he could in the trailer. He was alone
there after school one afternoon when Frankie and
Stewie came by.

"Why don't you make this place more comfortable?" Frankie complained. "This floor is too hard to sit on."

"I put my mattress down when I sleep here," Bruce said.

"Yeah, but it's not here now for just sitting. Can't you get some pillows out of your house?"

Bruce was thoughtful. Mrs. Logan had told him she was going to visit a neighbor down the street for a little while. She often did that in the afternoon.

"I'll see if the house is empty," he said to Frankie and Stewie. "You fellows wait here."

He went through the back door. No one was inside and he took the pillows off his bed and Robby's, carrying them to the trailer.

"How's this, fellows?" He tossed them inside.

"Not bad!" Frankie said, plumping a pillow behind his back. Then his eyes brightened. "Why don't we make this trailer really look good? Get a lot of things from both your house and mine."

"Like what?" Bruce asked with interest.

"Well, like food. And dishes and silverware. We could have a regular party in here. Wouldn't you like that?"

"Yep! Let's do it!" Bruce grew excited at the idea, but then he realized that he would get in trouble with Mrs. Logan if he took food from their ice box.

"Oh, we'll get it from mine! Come along!" Frankie said.

Frankie and Stewie's house was in its usual shambles but they managed to find some sardines, bread, bananas, plates, silverware and napkins. They marched back to the trailer and set themselves up for a party.

It had grown a bit dark out and Bruce said, "You know what would really be good in here?"

"What?" Stewie asked as he stripped a banana.

"Some light. Electricity. This would be really like a house then."

"How could we fix that up?" Frankie asked.

"Easy!" Bruce retorted. "I could bring a lamp in here. And we could get a lot of extension cords and connect them all together until they reached the house. Then we could plug it in through the window to my room."

"Let's do it!" Frankie leapt to his feet. "It'll be wonderful."

They ran to Bruce's house. He opened the door

73

cautiously to be sure that Mrs. Logan hadn't returned yet. It was quiet inside.

"There's an extension cord on this lamp." Bruce ran to a metal bridge lamp that stood next to a chair in the living room. He eyed the height of the lamp. It would fit into the trailer. "Let's take the whole thing!" he said, unplugging it from the wall socket.

They found extension cords all over the house, in the study, the bedrooms, the living room, and even in the kitchen.

"Why don't I connect one in my room first, and throw the other end out the window to you?" Bruce suggested.

He did just that, putting the plug in the wall and throwing the other end to Frankie who waited outside.

They connected cord after cord but when they had used the last one they were still a short distance away from the trailer.

"I'll get some from my house! You wait here with the lamp!" Frankie said.

He was back in a few seconds, more cords dangling from his hands. They hitched them up and with the last one just made it! They set the bridge lamp inside the trailer, turned it on—and it worked!

Light filled the trailer and Bruce lowered all the

flaps so that it was even snugger. It was as warm and cozy as an igloo.

"This is the way explorers must live!" he said to Frankie and Stewie.

"We're in the jungle!" Frankie took him up immediately.

"I hear lions and tigers roaring outside," Stewie added.

"We'd better eat our food before they smell it and come after us."

Never had a can of sardines tasted so delicious! The bread and fruit too. Bruce was swallowing a last mouthful when Stewie said, "I hear footsteps outside."

"Savages!" Frankie said. "A wild tribe. We'd better get our guns ready to shoot it out!"

Bruce heard the footsteps, too. He stood up as the flap opened. He expected to see Robby, or one of the Dickerson kids. Instead, there was Mrs. Logan. He was so startled that he took a step backward— and knocked the bridge lamp over!

It struck the floor of the trailer with a crash. The light went out—the bulb shattering with a loud sound!

"What are you boys up to in here? My kitchen clock has stopped and I noticed the lamp in the liv-

75

ing room was missing! Bruce—and you wild Indians—" She realized that Frankie and Stewie were here, too. "All of you—come out!"

"I'm not coming out!" Bruce felt afraid to leave the trailer. "I'm going to stay right here until Dad comes home. You're not going to spoil my fun—"

"You boys get out of here!" Mrs. Logan spoke so firmly to Frankie and Stewie that they grabbed some of their dishes and things and ran out of the trailer.

"What do you have in here—pillows, too?" Mrs. Logan reached for one. "Bruce, come along with me! Believe me, your dad is going to hear about this."

"I don't care! I'm not coming out! I don't have to do what you tell me. You're not my mother!"

Mrs. Logan didn't answer. She reached in, gripped Bruce by the arm and pulled him out of the trailer. At first he fell, with one knee on the ground, and he hurt himself. He didn't want to cry, but somehow he couldn't help it.

"You're not my mother! I don't have to do what you tell me!" he cried as Mrs. Logan led him into the house.

"I'm not your mother but you're going to learn to do what I tell you or I'm not going to stay on here!" Mrs. Logan exclaimed. She pushed Bruce toward his room. "Now you stay in there until your father comes home, and then we'll see what he has to say about this."

Bruce flung himself on the floor as he heard Mrs. Logan slam the door shut. Yes, he'd stay in here until Dad came home. And then he'd tell Dad how mean Mrs. Logan was, always bossing him, always trying to tell him what to do. He hated Mrs. Logan —he hated her! And if Dad didn't make Mrs. Logan go and get somebody else to take care of them— why—why he'd go away! He'd run to Grandma and Grandpa's and live there all the time, even without Robby or Dad.

He stayed in his room until he heard the car pull into the driveway. Then he ran into the living room to greet Dad.

Mrs. Logan was opening the door before him.

"Mr. Madison, I've been thinking things over," Mrs. Logan began even before Bruce had a chance to say "hello" to his father. "I've decided that I just can't manage the boys. I don't know whether it's my fault—or their fault—but they're just too much for me!"

Dad took off his hat and coat. "Now what's this all about?" he asked.

77

"It isn't so much Robby as Bruce. Somehow we two can't seem to manage to get along. He's always doing just the opposite of what I tell him and this afternoon I just stepped out of the house a moment—"

"I took some pillows from my room," Bruce interrupted her. "And Frankie and Stewie got some food and things from their house and we wanted a light so I took one of the lamps. It wouldn't have broken if Mrs. Logan hadn't scared me—"

"Scared him! I came home and could hardly find a light to turn on. The kitchen clock had stopped. Then I noticed a bridge lamp was missing and I saw a light in the trailer—"

"We took a lot of extension cords," Bruce said. "But I was going to bring them back when I came in for dinner."

"I think we'd better eat first and then talk this over more calmly," Dad said. "Where's Robby?"

"That's another thing," Mrs. Logan went on. "That boy just lives at the Dickersons'. You don't need me or anyone to take care of him. And if he is around he fights with Bruce. The two of them have made a nervous wreck out of me."

"Oh, now come!" Dad said. "They're not that bad!"

"You spoil them!" Mrs. Logan exclaimed. "That's another reason why I'm going to leave. You let them get away with anything they want. This job just isn't for me, Mr. Madison. I'm going to leave just as soon as you manage to find somebody else. In fact I'd like to go Monday morning—"

"Monday morning!" Dad was startled, because he saw that Mrs. Logan was really determined to leave. "How will I ever find anyone by Monday morning?"

"Well—I'll wait a few days longer. But not too much longer. And—and I'm too upset to have dinner with you tonight. Everything's on the stove—if you don't mind I'm going to my room."

Bruce was glad that Robby came in just then because Dad turned to him and asked, "Where have you been?"

"Next door—at the Dickersons'."

"The Dickersons'! Is this your home or is their place? Now wash up and I'll see what we have for dinner—"

"What's the matter?" Robby whispered as Bruce and he washed their hands in the bathroom.

"Oh, nothing! Except that I think Mrs. Logan's going to leave!" Bruce felt pleased about that.

"Mrs. Logan leave! Who'll take care of us?" Robby looked alarmed.

"We'll get somebody better. You didn't like her, did you?"

"A little. She makes such good cakes, too—"

"Yes, she did—" Bruce had to admit that as he returned to the dining room.

Dad had set dinner on the table. It was pot roast with potatoes and vegetables.

"I don't know whom we'll get if Mrs. Logan really leaves!" Dad said, his brow furrowed with concern. "And I don't know who's right—Mrs. Logan or you! It doesn't seem so awful that you borrowed a lamp but maybe she's right. Maybe I am too easy with you boys and spoil you! I don't know what we'll do if I can't get anybody to help us—"

"Can't we telephone Grandma? Can't she come down and take care of us?" Robby suggested.

"I don't know. I'll have to think about it! Bruce, you're going to be punished for this!" Dad suddenly looked stern. "You're going to your room right after dinner. Get into your pajamas and bed—"

"Not even look at TV?" Bruce groaned.

"Not even look at TV. And if the lamp or cords or anything are broken you're going to pay for them out of your allowance. Now finish your dinner and get to bed!"

Bruce didn't answer. He decided that Dad was

80

getting really angry now and it would be better not to say a word. He didn't mind going to bed early tonight. There wasn't anything much good to do anyway, and he was tired.

Mrs. Logan was in the kitchen at breakfast the next morning. She didn't have much to say but served breakfast to Bruce, Robby and Dad.

"I want to talk to you boys," Dad said before he left the house for work. He took them into his room.

"Mrs. Logan and I had a long talk late last night. She really wants to leave and I decided not to force her to stay. She's going to move to California to be near her son and his family. She wants to stop working for us at the end of the week—"

"But who'll take care of us if she goes?" Robby asked.

"I don't know. I'll have to start looking for a new housekeeper right away. I have to get to work now. Don't give Mrs. Logan any trouble—" Dad shot Bruce a warning glance.

Bruce was extra careful the rest of the week. Dad looked upset every evening when he came home. He said he was trying to find a housekeeper but couldn't locate anyone he really wanted.

When Saturday came around Mrs. Logan had her things all packed.

"I hate to leave you without anybody," she said to Dad at dinner that night. "But all my plans are made to go. I thought you'd surely have someone by now to take care of the house."

"Don't you worry. We'll manage somehow—" Dad said. He sounded as if, now that Mrs. Logan was going, he wasn't any more anxious to have her here than Bruce had been.

On Sunday morning Dad made breakfast for them. There was French toast but it was burnt quite a bit. Bruce didn't say anything though, pretending to like it.

Robby, however, refused to eat it. "It tastes awful! Who'll cook dinner for us tonight?"

"Mrs. Logan left some stew. You won't starve!" Dad sounded a bit cross.

"Who'll take care of us tomorrow when you go to work?" Robby persisted.

"I'll ask Mrs. Dickerson to look after you boys tomorrow until I get home."

"Can't we telephone Grandma?" Bruce asked. "She'd come down and help us."

"I guess she would—" Dad answered. He glanced at the clock on the wall. "She must be up now. I could telephone her and perhaps she and Grandpa would come down today and stay on until I find someone for the house."

Bruce was excited when Dad walked into the hall toward the phone. Mrs. Logan was gone and Grandma would be here in her place! That was better than anything he had ever hoped for! He saw Dad reach out for the telephone but then, to his surprise, Dad drew his hand back.

"No, I don't think I will call Grandma!" he was startled to hear his father say. "We're liable to get into trouble like this—without having anyone to take care of the house—lots of times! And we can't telephone Grandma, expect her to drop everything and come down whenever we get into some difficult spot. No—" Dad shook his head vehemently and returned to the kitchen. "We're going to pull through this on our own!"

Bruce couldn't help being disappointed. Why shouldn't they telephone Grandma when they were in trouble and have her come down to help them? What were grandmas and grandpas for? Grandma loved them and they loved her! But he knew from Dad's voice and the determined way he had returned to the kitchen that she wasn't going to be called!

"You know," Bruce said thoughtfully as he tackled the burnt French toast again, "Frankie and Stewie get along by themselves every day. Why couldn't Robby and I?"

"And have you two turn out to be the talk of the neighborhood, like those boys are?" Dad asked. "No, sir! Don't worry—I'll find somebody to take care of us!"

They pulled through the rest of that day fine but things were a bit strange around the house on Monday morning. It was a very different breakfast from the friendly one they had had with Dad on Sunday.

Bruce came into the kitchen, wearing his robe and slippers. Dad was standing at the stove, drinking a cup of coffee.

"Go right back to your room and get dressed!" Dad said. "See to it that Robby gets dressed, too. I want both of you ready for school before I leave the house."

From Dad's firm tone of voice Bruce knew that he'd better get dressed quickly. "Come on, Robby, stop playing and get your clothes on," he said.

"I don't want to get dressed yet," Robby said from the floor where he was playing with some soldiers.

"You have to! Come on, Dad will be angry!"

Bruce said, slipping into his clothes as quickly as he could.

"Oh, all right!" Robby grumbled.

"You boys will have to be content with just juice and cold cereal this morning." Dad motioned them to the kitchen table.

"I don't want cold cereal. Mrs. Logan always made me oatmeal!" Robby complained.

"I don't know how to make oatmeal and I don't have time anyway," Dad retorted. "Are your school bags ready? I think you'd better wear your warmer coats. The thermometer's way down this morning. I'm giving you Mrs. Logan's key to the house, Bruce. When you come home I want you boys to make up your beds and straighten your room. I'm making out a list of groceries and I'm leaving it with the money on the kitchen table. I want you to get the things when you come home from school. Hurry up now, both of you, or you'll be late!"

Bruce had never left the house in such a rush. One of his shoe laces was untied and he had to stop on the way to school to fasten it. His school bag fell open and all the contents tumbled to the ground.

He was glad to get to the classroom finally. It seemed so peaceful and quiet to him.

After school he walked home with Jimmy Dickerson.

"Are you going to play in the trailer?" Jimmy asked.

"Sure!" Bruce answered. "As soon as I tell Mrs. Logan I'm back—oh, I don't even have to do that!"

He left his schoolbag leaning against the back door. Jimmy and he had a fine time in the trailer, especially after some hot chocolate Jimmy brought out from his house.

"It's starting to get dark," Jimmy said later. "I'd better go in."

"Me, too. Dad will be along soon," Bruce said. He went to the back door and tried to open it. Then he remembered he had a key.

It was strange in the house without the sound of anyone there. He went to his room and suddenly realized that he hadn't made the bed after school, the way Dad wanted him to, or straightened up the room.

And the groceries! He ran into the kitchen, remembering about the things he was supposed to buy. There was the list and the money still on the table! He glanced at the clock on the wall. It was after five thirty! Dad would be home soon. Maybe

86

he'd just have time to run to the store and hurry back before Dad got home.

Never had Bruce reached the market so quickly. He managed to buy the groceries but couldn't rush back as fast loaded down with bundles.

His heart sank when he reached the house. There was Dad's car parked in the driveway.

"Hello, Bruce, I wondered where you were," Dad greeted him at the door.

"I—I forgot to get the groceries after school," Bruce confessed, "so I had to go for them now."

"I thought it might be something like that," Dad answered. "I found the house unlocked and empty. Robby was at the Dickersons', did you know that?"

"Well—I thought he might be—" Bruce answered. He went into the kitchen and deposited the groceries on the table. Robby was in the dining alcove, setting the table.

"But suppose Robby hadn't been at the Dickersons'," Dad went on. "Suppose something had happened to him. You're his older brother and should feel responsible for him—"

"I—I guess so—" was all Bruce could answer. He suddenly wondered if Dad had discovered that he hadn't made the beds or cleaned up. He started for his room.

87

"I hope you're going to make the beds now, Bruce." Dad's voice followed him. "Be sure you pick up everything from the floor, the toys, pajamas and robes—"

"Not Robby's things! He can do his own!"

"It won't hurt you to do a good job on the room by yourself. Robby's busy with something else. You know, I'm beginning to think that maybe Mrs. Logan was right. Perhaps I am too easy with you boys, inclined to spoil you. I want this room in ship-shape order by the time dinner is ready!"

Bruce stood alone in the middle of his room. And suddenly he thrust his foot out—kicking a toy automobile of Robby's clear across the room!

He wasn't spoiled! Mrs. Logan wasn't right about Dad being too easy with them. But as he got down on his hands and knees and started to pick up toys, old socks and pajamas from the floor, he almost wished that Mrs. Logan was still here—working for them.

Even though he hadn't liked her too much he had to admit that things had been better with her around.

SIX

Dad was very cheerful at breakfast the next morning.

"Fellows!" he said. "I have some good news for you. For all of us. Do you know that Mrs. Scofield who lives down the block?"

"I do!" Robby said. "She's the lady with the nice flower garden."

"Well, Mrs. Dickerson spoke to her about us. So last night both Mrs. Scofield and her husband came over and we worked out an arrangement together."

"You mean Mr. and Mrs. Scofield are going to move in here?" Bruce asked with surprise.

"Oh, no!" Dad laughed. "But Mrs. Scofield will come to clean the house in the morning every day. Then she'll go to her own house for a while and return in time to be here when you boys come back from school. I don't know how it will work out but we'll give it a trial."

Bruce had never known Mrs. Scofield too well, but he had always liked her. She was in the kitchen when he came home from school that afternoon, busy preparing dinner.

"Hello, Bruce! Have a good day in school?" She smiled at him.

It seemed strange not to have Mrs. Logan here. And somehow, Mrs. Scofield's questions reminded him of Mom, the way she used to greet him when he came home.

"Are you hungry? Would you like a glass of milk? Or an apple? Can you just help yourself?" Mrs. Scofield had a cheerful smile.

Bruce took a glass of milk and then started for the back yard.

"I'll leave the back door open," she called. The plan was for her to go home after she got dinner ready and the boys would wait for their father by themselves.

When Bruce returned from playing with Jimmy, he turned on the lights. Even though Robby and he looked at television he didn't like this time of waiting in the house alone. He kept thinking he heard Dad's car coming up the driveway, but it always turned out to be someone else going along the street.

"I'm hungry!" Robby announced as one of the programs showed a lady mixing a pudding.

"You can take something out of the ice box," Bruce said. "Mrs. Logan isn't here to stop you."

He heard another car and this time he knew it was Dad! Both Robby and he were at the door as Dad came in.

"I don't like waiting all alone!" Robby cried.

"I don't either!" Bruce added.

"I'm a little late, fellows," Dad apologized. "But I couldn't help it. The traffic was so heavy tonight. Are you as hungry as I am? Let's see what Mrs. Scofield left for us."

There was a rich stew for dinner, and afterward Bruce and Robby helped Dad clean up the kitchen.

As the days went on the boys began to get used to the new arrangement. It gave Bruce a feeling of being on his own which he enjoyed. Robby still liked to go to the Dickersons' and after Mrs. Scofield went home, Bruce would sometimes hang around the street, always sure of finding Frankie and Stewie there.

The weather had turned really cold and winter was here for sure, Bruce knew, the day it snowed.

The first snow didn't stay on the ground very long.

"I wish it would snow again!" Bruce sighed longingly to Frankie and Stewie one afternoon. "Then we could build a fort and have a real snow fight."

"Snow never lasts long enough," Frankie said. "Why don't we make ourselves some slingshots? They can't ever melt away!"

Bruce liked that idea. The leaves were off all the trees and it was easy finding Y-shaped pieces of wood to make slingshots.

Frankie knew how to make them expertly. He had strong pieces of rubber at home for bands and even pieces of leather for the pouches.

"Let's be a club!" Frankie exclaimed. "Let's practice and practice and then we can be the 'Sure-Shots'!"

They started practicing in Frankie and Stewie's back yard, aiming stones at a tin can set on a fence. Bruce was surprised at how good a shot he turned out to be. Plop! He hardly ever missed knocking the can over!

"I wish we could find something better to shoot at!" Frankie complained.

"How about that house?" Bruce motioned to one down the street. "The people who live in it went on a vacation to Florida last week."

He was only half-serious but Frankie took him up on it.

"Let's see who can hit the closest to that window over the door without really hitting it!" Frankie said. He lifted his slingshot and sent a stone whirring through the air. It bounded against the window sill and then fell to the ground.

"Gee, suppose we should hit a window and break it!" Bruce said.

"They won't know who did it. Come on—don't be scared!"

They were standing in a gravel driveway and Bruce found a stone, pulled his slingshot taut, and hit the sill even closer to the window than Frankie had. Stewie also took a turn but he made a bad shot.

"You can't be in the Sure-Shot Club unless you do better than that!" Frankie said. He aimed again but didn't do very well and Stewie hooted. "*Who* won't be in the club?"

"Looks like I'm the champ so far!" Bruce said proudly. He picked up a good stone, aimed at the sill again and then— *Cr—as—sh!*

His heart seemed to go to pieces at the same time that the window went shattering to the ground.

"Come on—we'd better beat it!" Frankie cried,

93

starting to run toward his house. Bruce and Stewie were at his heels.

"Boys—you come back here—!" Bruce heard a voice calling after them but he didn't know who it was. He didn't bother to look either. He just kept running—running!

"So long—see you tomorrow—" he called as he ran to his house, leaving Frankie and Stewie to go to theirs.

Mrs. Scofield must have gone home because the place was dark and empty. For a moment he didn't turn any light on at all. Had the person who called after them recognized either him, Frankie or Stewie? It had been getting dark so maybe they didn't know who had broken that window. If Dad found out he would really be angry, Bruce knew that.

He tried not to think about it when Robby came home and a little later, Dad.

"Did you boys get along all right today? What did Mrs. Scofield leave for our dinner?"

"We—we got along fine—" Bruce answered. "I don't know what Mrs. Scofield left."

It was some very good chicken but Bruce didn't have much appetite for it. He kept worrying that the doorbell or telephone would ring at any minute and it would be someone telling Dad what he had done to that window.

The telephone did ring—it was just a friend of Dad's—but Bruce had some worrisome moments before he knew that. Then, while Dad was still on the phone, the front doorbell rang.

"Bruce, will you answer that?" Dad called from the phone.

Bruce opened the door and Mrs. Adamson, Nancy's mother, stood there.

"Hello, Bruce. Is your father in? I'd like to talk to him."

What did she want? He hadn't done anything to Nancy.

"My—my dad's on the phone—" Bruce said, but Mrs. Adamson walked right in.

"Hello!" Dad had finished his conversation and came smiling toward Mrs. Adamson. "How are you? I haven't seen you or your husband for a long time."

"We've been around but we don't get out so much in this weather," Mrs. Adamson said. "Last time I came here was because Bruce and those wild boys had turned the hose on Nancy, remember?"

Bruce felt his heart quicken as Mrs. Adamson went on.

"I hate to be the one who's always reporting on

Bruce. But Mr. and Mrs. Baldwin who live next door to me are in Florida and they asked me to keep an eye on their house. Well, I was in the kitchen getting dinner ready and I heard a crash. I went to the back door and I saw three boys running away. They'd broken one of the upstairs windows in the Baldwin house. I couldn't be positive the boys were Bruce and those other two wild ones, but I just have a feeling that's who they were!"

Mrs. Adamson stopped talking and Bruce felt Dad and her looking at him. He could say he hadn't been there because Mrs. Adamson hadn't said positively that she had seen him. But he felt his face burning and Dad's eyes on him. He had never been able to lie very easily—

"I—I—we weren't trying to break any windows! We were aiming at the sill with our slingshots—trying not to hit the windows—just get close—and I'd hit the sill before, but this time—"

"Slingshots are dangerous weapons. Your mother and I both told you that a long, long time ago!"

Bruce felt tears well up in his eyes. Why—why did Dad have to talk about Mom in front of Mrs. Adamson?

"I know you have a hard time bringing up the boys," Mrs. Adamson went on. "But you must admit

I warned you a long time ago against letting Bruce play with those fellows across the street. I'll have the Baldwin window fixed and I'm afraid I'll have to send you the bill, Mr. Madison." Mrs. Adamson started for the door.

"You do that," Dad said. "The money will come out of Bruce's allowance."

Dad turned to Bruce after Mrs. Adamson left. He was really angry.

"Bruce, you're going to be punished for this! I—I sometimes feel I ought to take you over my knee and give you an old-fashioned spanking! You'll pay for the window! You won't be able to look at a single television program for two weeks! And if I ever catch you with those two boys—Frankie and Stewie again—well—well, I don't know what I'll do! But you won't like it, I can tell you that much!"

It was hard to keep Frankie and Stewie away. They kept coming over and Bruce had to say, "My father won't let me play with you. I—I guess we just get into too much trouble when we're together. So beat it! Go away and let me alone!"

"Who wants to play with you anyway?" Frankie sniffed, pulling Stewie with him as they went back to their side of the street. But somehow Bruce knew he had hurt Frankie's feelings and he felt badly about it.

"Do you fellows know that it will be Christmas before too long?" Dad asked them at dinner one night. "What would you rather do? Go to Grandma and Grandpa's for a visit or have them come here?"

"Oh, let's go there!" Bruce exclaimed. "We haven't been there in such a long time."

"Yes, I'd like that!" Robby agreed and Dad said he'd arrange it.

Suddenly the world took on its "just-before-Christmas" look. Santa Claus appeared in all the magazines and newspapers. A big tree with lights stood in Clayton Park. The store windows and streets glittered with holiday decorations. Everybody sang Christmas songs on radio and television. The children started making presents in school.

"We're going to make pot-holders for our mothers and paperweights for our fathers," Miss Hayden, Bruce's teacher, said.

Bruce felt some of the children glancing at him, knowing that he didn't have a mother to give a pot-holder to. Miss Hayden recalled that, also, as she handed out the materials.

"Why don't you make it for your grandmother?" she suggested with a kindly smile.

Bruce just nodded, agreeing, but he didn't like feeling and being different from everyone else in the class.

A few days before Christmas Dad looked at both boys and said, "Bruce, you don't need a haircut but Robby, you certainly do. I don't know when I'll have time to take you. Do you think you could go to the barber with him after school, Bruce?"

"Oh, I was going to play with Jimmy!" Bruce complained.

"I wonder if you couldn't go for a haircut by yourself." Dad looked at Robby. "Do you think you'd like to try it?"

"You mean to the barber shop next to the supermarket? Where all the stores are?" Robby asked.

"That's right. You only have one big street to cross and there's a traffic light at the corner. I'll give you the money and you could just go into the barber shop and ask for a haircut."

Bruce watched Robby thinking it over. He was almost tempted to say, "Oh, all right, I won't play with Jimmy, I'll take him," because most kids as little as Robby didn't go for haircuts alone. They—they had mothers to take them. But before he had a chance to speak Robby answered.

100

"All right! I'll go by myself!" He held his hand out for the money.

Bruce had fun at the Dickersons' after school. They played with Jimmy's electric trains and afterwards Linda came in with a girl named Peggy and they all played together. Phil kept asking when Robby would be back from the barber shop.

Robby finally appeared.

"Look!" He proudly whisked his cap off his head. "The man put some stuff on my hair. Smell it!"

Robby's hair was freshly cut and everybody leaned over to smell it. It smelled beautiful and Bruce was proud of Robby.

"He went to the barber's all alone! At his age!" he told everyone proudly.

After a while Mrs. Dickerson let the girls make some hot chocolate which they all had in Jimmy and Phil's room. Everyone began to talk about Christmas and what they wanted.

"I want a new fishing rod!" Bruce announced. "A really good one with a basket and all the equipment."

"In the winter!" Jimmy sniffed. "What will you do with it all winter?"

"I'll keep it until spring. But I want it now." Bruce was insistent.

101

"Will Mommy be mad if we have a good time on Christmas without her?" Robby suddenly asked.

Bruce was so startled that he almost spilled his hot chocolate. He wished that Robby hadn't mentioned Mom in front of everybody. He was surprised, too, because he thought that Robby hardly ever worried or thought about Mom.

It was Linda who answered first. She said, "Your Mommy's an angel in heaven and can see everything. She'll be glad if you have a good time."

"What happens to you after you're dead and they bury you?" Phil asked.

"You just turn into dust, like the ground, and pretty trees and flowers grow," Peggy, Linda's friend, put in. "That's what my daddy told me happens to you after you die."

"My—my grandmother says that happens to your body." Bruce was surprised to find himself able to talk about it. "But that your—your soul—goes to heaven—"

"Anybody in here want some more hot chocolate?" Mrs. Dickerson came into the room. "There's a spot more left in the pot."

Peggy and Jimmy took more and then they talked about Christmas again and the things they wanted for gifts. After a while Peggy said she had to go

102

home. Bruce decided that Robby and he had better leave, too.

When they reached the house Robby turned on the television. Bruce wasn't allowed to look at it yet, as punishment for breaking the window. He kept his promise to Dad, usually reading or playing in his room instead. Today, however, he wandered by himself into Dad's room.

Mom's picture stood there in the silver frame. Bruce usually turned his eyes away from it. But somehow, after talking about Mom—because that was who they had really been talking about in Jimmy's room, he knew—he found himself looking at Mom's picture. It wasn't hard. He didn't have that sharp, stabbing pain he usually had when he tried to look at it.

Mom was smiling at him and he found himself leaning close to the picture, whispering, "It's all right if we have a nice Christmas, isn't it?" And Mom seemed to say, "Oh, yes, you and Robby have a wonderful Christmas!"

SEVEN

They drove up to Grandma and Grandpa's house the day before Christmas, the heater on in the car to keep them warm. As they rode they sang, starting with *Jingle Bells,* then *Silent Night, I'm Dreaming of a White Christmas* and *Rudolph, the Red-Nosed Reindeer.*

Grandma and Grandpa were at the door almost the moment the car pulled up to the house. After hugs and kisses Bruce and Robby ran up to the room where they had slept during the summer. It was good to see it again, but it looked smaller to Bruce and kind of old-fashioned.

Bruce explored the outdoors, too, the trees he used to climb, the streets he roamed and he found some of the old friends he had made last summer.

The boys hung up their stockings before they went to bed. Grandma had a slim little red book with *The Night Before Christmas* in gold letters on the cover. She told them she had had this same book since she was a little girl. She read them the poem and then Robby and Bruce hopped into bed.

"I hope I get my fishing rod!" Bruce said to Dad.

"I hope you do, too!" Dad said which worried Bruce a bit. Why didn't Dad say, "I'm sure you will!"

Robby had his heart set on a whole family of little stuffed bears he had seen in a shop window.

Of course the boys were the first ones up in the house the next morning, scampering down the stairs.

"I got them! I got them!" Robby cried, seeing his whole bear family sitting in a row.

"My rod, too!" Bruce exclaimed happily, because what else could be in that tall, thin package? Beside the beautiful fishing rod there were gleaming ice-skates from Grandpa and Grandma.

Bruce gave Grandma the pot-holder he had made and Grandpa a necktie and Dad the paperweight and Robby a top that made designs when it spun round. There were books and games and wind-up automobiles and enough presents to make both boys happy.

Roast turkey with stuffing, cranberry sauce and mince pie! That was dinner later in the day. Bruce

ate so much, especially stuffing which he loved, that he thought he would burst.

After dinner the grown ups sat around the table, still talking, while the boys made a line-up of trucks on the floor, pushing them around.

"Are things working out all right with Mrs. Scofield taking care of the boys?" Grandma was asking Dad.

"Pretty well," Dad answered. "Though I wish I

could find someone good and steady to live in the
house. I worry about the boys being left on their
own too much."

"Do you remember an old friend of mine, Mrs.
Fowler?" Grandma asked. "She works at Red Cross
on Saturdays as I do. She lives alone and is thinking
of taking some kind of job. I told her about you
and the boys and she sounded a little bit interested."

"She's a nice woman!" Dad exclaimed. "Do you
think I could talk to her while I'm here?"

"I don't want to bother her on Christmas Day," Grandma said. "But we could phone her tomorrow. Of course, son, the best thing for you and the boys would be for you to get married again."

Bruce had been listening to Dad and his grandparents talking as he pushed one of the toy automobiles. He heard Dad laugh now and say, "Well, I don't feel ready to get married yet. I do take someone out once in a while, Helen Gorman. She's the person who gave the boys the trailer they have in the back yard."

Bruce was surprised to hear that. He didn't know that Dad still saw Mrs. Gorman. Why hadn't Dad told him about it?

The next morning Dad and Grandma went to see the lady who might be interested in a housekeeping job. When Dad came back he said that Mrs. Fowler was very nice but that she wasn't sure she wanted to move out of town. She would think it over and let him know.

The plan was for Bruce and Robby to spend all their Christmas vacation at their grandparents'. Dad would go home and call for them next weekend.

It was a busy week for the boys. Bruce went ice skating on a pond near Grandma's every day. Once

108

they went downtown to a movie, but mostly they had a wonderful time just playing outdoors.

The next weekend Dad came for them. On Saturday afternoon when Bruce came into the living room a lady was sitting there whom he had never seen before.

"Bruce, this is my good friend, Mrs. Fowler," Grandma said.

"Mrs. Fowler has decided to work for us and to be our new housekeeper," Dad explained. "Isn't that nice?"

"How old are you, Bruce?" Mrs. Fowler asked. "I have a grandson who is just about your age, I think."

"I'm ten, going on eleven," Bruce answered. He was examining Mrs. Fowler closely. She had lots of wrinkles on her face but she didn't look old. Her eyes were bright and twinkly, and she had a wide, friendly smile.

"Mrs. Fowler and I have known each other since we were little girls," Grandma said. "I'm going to feel so much better knowing that she'll be taking care of you."

They started for home early Sunday, stopping at Mrs. Fowler's house to pick her up. She had several suitcases and a large, odd-looking black one.

"What's in there?" Robby asked, as he sat in the back seat with Mrs. Fowler.

"It's a guitar," Mrs. Fowler answered.

Bruce, who was sitting up front with Dad, turned around with excitement. "Do you play it?" he asked.

"Yes, I do." Mrs. Fowler smiled. "I'll play it for you sometime soon."

When they reached home Mrs. Fowler admired their house from the outside, and was even more pleased with her room. The boys coaxed her to show them the guitar, which she did. It was beautiful, shiny and honey-colored, and she let them twang the strings.

"I'll have to fix something so I can hang it on the wall," she said. "I like my guitar hanging on the wall, because then it's so easy to take down."

Bruce and Robby ran over to the Dickersons' and saw Jimmy, Linda, Phil and Taffy, as well as all the nice things they had received for presents.

When they returned home Mrs. Fowler was bustling about in the kitchen and it was a nice sound to Bruce's ears. Supper was good and afterwards the boys begged Mrs. Fowler to play the guitar.

"Suppose you get into your pajamas and I'll sing you some good-night songs," she said.

They were in their pajamas almost as quickly as

you could say "Guitar!" Mrs. Fowler sat on a chair in their room, the guitar in her lap. Dad stood in the doorway, too, as she sang.

> *A yankee ship came down the river,*
> > *Blow, boys, blow,*
> *Her masts and spars they shone like silver,*
> > *Blow, my bully boys, blow.*

She sang other songs, too, about frogs, cowboys and babies, but Bruce liked the "Blow, boys, blow" one the best.

He told Jimmy about Mrs. Fowler's singing on the way to school the next day, and promised he'd get her to sing for him sometime.

Bruce saw Frankie and Stewie in the school yard. He waved to them, because he really wasn't mad at them, but he was determined to keep away from them. He didn't want to give Mrs. Fowler any trouble.

Things went smoothly in the house for several weeks. The boys didn't even mind when Dad went out evenings, because it was so nice to be home with Mrs. Fowler. She started to teach Bruce how to pluck at the guitar and play what almost sounded like a tune.

One night during the week Dad asked at the din-

111

ner table, "Mrs. Fowler, do you think you could bake us an apple pie for Sunday. I'm having some company in for dinner and your pie is so good."

Mrs. Fowler always took Sunday off and spent it with various friends she knew in town.

"Who's coming on Sunday?" Robby asked.

"You remember Helen Gorman, don't you?" Dad answered. "I invited her for dinner."

"I thought we'd do something on Sunday," Bruce exclaimed. "Like go to the movies or visit somebody."

"Not this Sunday." Dad shook his head. "It'll be nice to have company for a change."

Bruce felt a bit disappointed but not as bad as he did when Jimmy told him that he was going to the movies on Sunday.

"They're showing a new picture about Robin Hood downtown," Jimmy said. "They say it's swell!"

"Oh, I can't miss that!" Bruce cried. But when he spoke to Dad about it, Dad shook his head in a positive manner. "I'm sorry, we're not going to the movies this Sunday. You'll have to see it some other time."

"But there isn't any other time. Can't I go with the Dickersons if they'll take me?"

112

"No, I want you at home. You'll be able to see the picture some other day."

"You won't let me go during the week when there's school!" Bruce persisted.

"Well, it'll be at another theater. I promise to take you one day so let's not discuss it any more."

Bruce felt worse on Sunday. He was playing with Jimmy in the early afternoon when all the Dickersons came out of their house.

"Come on, Jimmy, we're all ready to go to the movie now!"

Bruce saw them drive off, then he started toward his house, kicking a stone along the way. Everybody had a good time except him! He opened the back door and then he heard the sound of laughter.

For a moment he thought it was Mrs. Fowler— but then he saw it was a strange lady. She was in the kitchen and she was cooking something on the stove. Dad was standing beside her, smiling.

"Here's Bruce now," Dad said. "Bruce, you remember Mrs. Gorman, don't you?"

"Why—why yes—" Bruce said, though Mrs. Gorman looked different to him. Somehow she didn't seem as nice though she was pretty with blonde hair and a silver pin on her dress.

"Of course we remember each other!" Mrs. Gorman said. "I'm helping your father get dinner ready. Are you as hungry as I am, Bruce?"

"I—I guess so—" Bruce answered. He noticed that Mrs. Gorman was wearing Mrs. Fowler's apron. What was she doing that for? Why did she have to come into the kitchen anyway? Dad and he could get dinner ready without her butting in. Besides, if it wasn't for her, he might be at the movies now, enjoying *Robin Hood*.

Bruce tried to be polite at the dinner table, but he didn't like Dad and Mrs. Gorman talking together so much. When they finished eating he went into his room and got out his copy of *Robin Hood*.

He was stretched out on the floor, when Mrs. Gorman came in.

"I'm leaving now, Bruce. I just want to say good-bye—"

"Oh—good-bye—" He hardly looked up at her.

"I don't suppose you can use the trailer much in this weather." Mrs. Gorman's voice was so soft and nice that Bruce couldn't help being less angry. He had almost forgotten that she had given him the trailer.

"No, I can't use it now. But I had a wonderful time in it."

"And you will again when the weather turns

114

warm. It was nice being with you. Good-bye, Bruce!"

He decided he wasn't so angry at her—not the way he was at Dad. When he returned to the living room Dad spoke sharply to him.

"You didn't behave very well today, Bruce. You looked and sounded grumpy all afternoon. That's no way to act when we have company."

"I don't care!" he answered boldly.

"Maybe you don't. Or maybe you're just angry because I didn't let you go to the movies," Dad answered. "But just to make sure that you behave better next time we have guests I'm not going to take you to see that picture, even when it does come to another theater."

"Then you're a—a—" Bruce, in a sudden rage, couldn't think of a name bad enough to call his father. Instead he ran to his room and slammed the door shut.

Dad didn't say anything more to him, not even later when Bruce came out for a bite of supper. And when Dad leaned over his bed to kiss him good night, Bruce turned away, pulling the covers over his head so his father couldn't reach him.

The next morning, on the way to school, Jimmy

told Bruce all about the movie and how wonderful it had been.

Bruce hardly paid attention to his work in class. He still felt mad at Dad for not taking him to see *Robin Hood*. And now he wasn't sure he would get to see it ever!

As he walked home from school he saw Frankie and Stewie up ahead. He had kept away from them for a long time but suddenly he walked faster, catching up to them.

"Hello, fellows, where are you going?" he asked.

Frankie looked up at him, as if not sure he wanted to talk to Bruce after he had kept away so long. But then he relented and said, "We're just trying to think of something to do."

"I know what I'd like to do," Bruce said.

"What?" Stewie asked.

"Go see *Robin Hood* at the movies. I wanted to see it yesterday but my father wouldn't take me."

"We wanted to go, too!" Frankie exclaimed. "But our folks said they were too tired to do anything. Say!" His eyes lit up. "Why don't we go now?"

"Now!" Bruce's eyes widened. "It's too late. We'd have to go all the way downtown. Besides—I don't have any money—"

"We have money!" Frankie dug his hand into his

116

pocket and drew out a dollar bill and some silver. "We'll lend you some money. We could take the bus downtown and go to the movies!"

Bruce stared at the money in Frankie's hand. He'd never been to the movies downtown alone. It would be wonderful to go by bus and see *Robin Hood!*

"All right! Let's do it!" he said.

Bruce had never been downtown without a grown up. It was exciting to board the bus, ride toward the downtown section, and then walk along the street. Frankie, Stewie and he all kept close together through the crowds. They came to the moving picture theater and there were the posters proclaiming *The Adventures of Robin Hood* in shiny, gold letters, with a picture of Robin Hood and his men holding their bows and arrows high.

Frankie went right up to the window where the lady sold tickets and bought three of them. Bruce had been in this theater many times. It was big and beautiful with thick carpet on the floor and a counter that sold candy and popcorn.

"I want some popcorn!" Stewie cried.

"We can each have something for ten cents," Frankie said.

The popcorn was fifteen cents so Bruce and Stewie decided to put their money together. They

117

bought one package of popcorn and a package of licorice sticks with the money they had left, plus a penny Bruce found in his pocket. Then they went into the main part of the theater.

The picture was on and the boys could hardly bring themselves to find seats, walking down the aisle watching the screen. There was Robin Hood himself, in his green suit and hat, arguing with a man about crossing a river.

"Here—I think there are three seats in here—" Bruce said and they all slid into a row.

For an hour and a half they sat, putting candy and popcorn into their mouths until it was all gone, and still keeping their mouths open as the picture went on.

It was as good as the book with some things that hadn't even been in the book! If only he could have lived in those days, Bruce thought, and belonged to the band in Sherwood Forest!

"I'm glad we came in the middle," Frankie said, when the picture ended. "We can stay and see the end of it over again."

"Won't that be too late?" Bruce asked with sudden concern. For a while he had forgotten that he had come to the movies without Dad, Mrs. Fowler, or anyone knowing.

"Oh, it wasn't such a long picture," Frankie reassured him.

There was a newsreel and a funny cartoon. Then Bruce became interested in *Robin Hood* again and they sat through it right up to the end.

"Gosh, it's dark out!" Bruce exclaimed when they reached the street.

They rushed to the bus stop and a bus came along quickly. Bruce began to get scared when he saw a clock in a store window. It was after eight! He had thought it was late—but not so late! Dad would be madder than ever—and where would he say he had been?

"So long!" Frankie and Stewie left Bruce as soon as they got off the bus, hurrying to their house.

Bruce walked to the back door, his heart pounding loudly, his teeth digging into his bottom lip. What would he say to his father—what excuse could he give?

"Bruce! Bruce is here!" He heard Robby's voice first as he entered. And then he was startled by the number of people assembled in the kitchen.

Robby, and Mrs. Fowler and Dad, and Mrs. Dickerson with Jimmy and Linda and Phil—

"Bruce, are you all right? Bruce—where have you been?" Dad came toward him.

119

"I—I'm fine—I—I didn't know—it was so late—" he managed to stammer.

"Where were you until this hour? We've called the whole neighborhood!" Mrs. Fowler looked worried, too.

"They even told the police!" Robby put in.

"I—I—" Bruce felt his face turning hot. He couldn't lie about it. "I—I went to the movies—with Frankie and Stewie—and they made me stay through the picture twice. I didn't know it was so late."

"What did you see?" Jimmy asked with eager interest.

"*Robin Hood*—it was swell—" The words just came to Bruce's lips and then he noticed the expression that had come over Dad's face.

"If you don't mind, I'd like to see Bruce alone," Dad said, in a voice that seemed far away and strange to Bruce.

"We'd better be getting home, anyway." Mrs. Dickerson steered Jimmy, Linda and Phil to the back door. "I left Mr. Dickerson with the baby—"

Bruce felt Dad's hand on his arm the moment the door closed behind the Dickersons.

"You get back to bed, Robby!" Dad's voice was firm. He was leading Bruce into the study, his fingers

120

gripping so tightly that Bruce winced with pain. He tried to pull away but Dad only tightened his hold.

"Ow—you're hurting me—" Bruce cried.

Dad closed the door of the study behind them.

"I don't know what I ought to do about you, Bruce," Dad exclaimed. "I think I really ought to spank you this time! You know that I had forbidden you to go to that movie! You not only went but stayed so late—I—I ought to give you a good wallop with a hairbrush—or—or something—" Dad let go of Bruce's arm with a push that sent him sprawling across his father's bed.

Sobs choked Bruce's throat. He didn't like his dad talking to him this way. And suddenly words came to his lips, escaping between sobs.

"Mommy—Mommy—I want—my mommy—"

"Bruce—stop that! Stop calling for Mommy!" He felt his father sit beside him on the bed. Then Mr. Madison pulled him up, holding Bruce by the arms so that he had to face him.

"Bruce, Mommy isn't here! You can't go on calling for her to help you! Bruce, when Mommy first died, I told you to cry if it would make you feel better, didn't I? But the time's come now when we have to stop crying for her every time we get into

121

a jam. We have to accept the fact that she's gone for good and that we can only depend on ourselves."

There was something about Dad's voice, the grown-up way in which he was talking, that made Bruce catch his breath, look directly at his father.

"Bruce, do you realize how worried I was about you tonight?" Dad went on. "But I don't blame you entirely for what happened. I blame myself, too. I didn't let you go to the movie Sunday because we had company. I said you could see it another time. But then I lost my temper and said you couldn't see it at all, which really wasn't fair of me. But it's hard to always know what's right. Sometimes—I feel so badly"—Bruce saw Dad hesitating for the right words—"that I want to cry out, 'Mommy! Mommy!', too."

Bruce looked at Dad, who seemed to be talking to him in a grown-up way that he never had used before.

"Sometimes I get tired, scared and lonely, too," Dad went on. "I feel—as if I don't know how to bring you boys up the way Mom would have liked. I don't do or say the right things. I spoil Robby and you or else I'm too strict. You see—it's just as hard for me to try and be a good father—as it is for you to be a good son."

122

Bruce stared at his father and suddenly all that Dad had been saying seemed clear to him.

He hadn't realized—that Dad was having such a hard time! He had thought that Dad—was just Dad —he didn't know that a father had to worry about whether he was a good one or not.

"I—I'll try to be better!" he gulped, not wanting to cry, trying to be brave for Dad now. "I'll try to be better—by myself—without—calling for Mommy —or anyone."

"I'll try to be better, too!" Dad said. He put his arm around Bruce and they both went inside.

EIGHT

"What did your father do to you last night?" Jimmy asked Bruce on the way to school the next morning.

"Oh—we—I got off easy—" Bruce said, though he didn't mean that. But he couldn't tell Jimmy about it. What had happened was private, just between his father and himself.

After school he met Frankie and Stewie.

"Did we get it!" Frankie said. "We have to stay in the house or the back yard after school. We can't go any place else, even to your side of the street."

Bruce didn't mind that. In fact he was glad to hear it. It would be easier to keep away from Frankie and Stewie then.

He stayed pretty close to the house himself for the next few weeks. One afternoon Mrs. Fowler baked a chocolate cake when he came in from school and she let him mix the frosting as well as lick the spoon and bowl.

Another afternoon it began to snow during school hours and it was quite deep by the time Bruce started for home.

"Come on into our yard and we'll build a snow fort!" Frankie urged Bruce.

It sounded like fun but Bruce was afraid to start up with Frankie and Stewie again. As Jimmy had said when he first came back from Grandma's last summer, "somehow you always end up in trouble with them."

"I—I've got something else to do," he said to Frankie, running on home.

He built a snowman with Jimmy in the back of the house.

Later in the afternoon Mrs. Fowler took down her guitar and sang for Robby and him. Bruce loved Mrs. Fowler's songs and could never hear enough of them.

There was wonderful sled riding on Hanover Street hill all the next week. But by Monday the weather turned warmer and the snow melted away.

"The weatherman said we might have some more snow though," Mrs. Fowler said at breakfast a few days later. "I hope not. I have to go downtown to the dentist this afternoon. Do you boys remember that I said I could only get a late appointment? You'll have to let yourselves into the house after school."

"Oh, that's all right!" Bruce answered. "We used to do it all the time when Mrs. Scofield was here—"

"What time is your appointment?" Dad asked Mrs. Fowler.

"At four o'clock. I ought to be home by five-thirty easily."

"Well, why don't you stay downtown until I'm finished work and I can drive you home," Dad suggested.

"That would be just grand!" Mrs. Fowler beamed. "The buses are so crowded at that hour with everyone coming home from work."

Bruce was working on his notebook in school that afternoon when someone in class blurted out, "Look, it's snowing again!"

"Hooray!" someone else shouted and the teacher had to rap for order.

The snow fell like a lacy curtain over the window all the rest of the school hours.

"It's not hard enough yet for sled riding." Jimmy plowed through it on the way home.

126

"But it's swell for packing!" Bruce answered.

It seemed to get dark earlier than usual tonight, because the sky was so gray and the snow still coming down so hard. When Bruce and Robby let themselves into the house they had to put dry clothes on immediately.

"When's Mrs. Fowler coming?" Robby asked, his nose pressed against the window.

"She's driving with Dad. They ought to be here by six," Bruce said.

In the middle of a cowboy chase something went wrong with the television set. It looked as if snow were coming right through, on to the picture. The boys turned the set off and went into their room.

"Boy, this looks like the most snow yet!" Robby said with excitement.

Bruce went to the window, too. It was dark now, with only the yellow street lights making a glow outside. Flakes danced around the lights, the way moths did in the summer. All around, the houses, trees, sidewalks, everything was white with snow.

"It looks like fairyland!" Bruce exclaimed but then he began to worry. There wasn't a soul on the street, nor even a car coming along. He wondered if Dad would get through all right.

"Why isn't Dad home?" Robby asked, as if thinking the same thing.

"Oh, he won't be long—" Bruce tried to reassure him.

He was happy when the phone rang a few minutes later. It was Dad!

"Bruce, I had a bit of trouble locating the dentist's office where Mrs. Fowler is. We're both there now. We're leaving for home but it may take a little while because the snow's coming down so hard. Are you fellows all right?"

"Oh, yes, we're fine!" Bruce answered.

Both Robby and he felt better after that. They

128

played some checkers, although Robby wasn't too good at it. He was always more interested in counting how many checkers he had piled up.

"I'm hungry!" Robby announced before the game was over.

"I am, too!" Bruce agreed. "Let's see what we can find."

They each had a glass of milk and a piece of bread. Bruce flopped down on the floor in his room to read a while after he had eaten.

"I'm still hungry." Robby stood in the doorway.

"So am I!" Bruce realized how hollow his stomach felt. He got to his feet and went back to the kitchen. It was almost eight o'clock! Why weren't Dad and Mrs. Fowler home? He went to the kitchen and peered out. It was snowing harder than ever—the whole world was white!

"I bet they can't get through the snow!" Bruce exclaimed.

"You mean they're never coming home?" Robby asked with alarm.

"Oh, I don't mean that!" Bruce reassured him. "But maybe they'll have to wait for the snow plows to clear the roads."

"I don't want to stay here. I want to go next door to the Dickersons'," Robby cried.

"No, I think we ought to wait here," Bruce said. "Dad might be along any minute."

When the doorbell rang, Bruce was surprised. He hadn't heard the car pull into the garage. But maybe it wouldn't make any noise on the soft snow. He hurriedly opened the door.

"Hello—can we come in?" He was startled to see not Dad and Mrs. Fowler—but Frankie and Stewie!

"What are you doing here?" he cried.

"Our father and mother haven't come home yet," Frankie said. "And something's wrong with the heat in our house. I went down cellar but the oil burner doesn't seem to be making any noise—"

"We're so cold!" Stewie put in. His teeth were chattering and his eyes were filled with tears.

They did look cold, both of them. They had their coats, hats and boots on, and they were covered with snow. There was even snow on Frankie's eyelashes. But should he let them in here? Bruce wondered. He wasn't even supposed to play with them.

"Please, can't we come in?" Frankie pleaded, in a way that didn't sound like him at all.

"Come—come on in—" Bruce said. He couldn't send them into all that snow—back to their cold house. "Take your things off right here. You're dripping water—"

130

Frankie and Stewie peeled off their coats, hats and boots and then stood in front of the living room radiator, trying to get warm.

"How'll your father and mother know you're here if they do come home?" Bruce asked.

"Oh, we left a note saying where we were," Frankie answered. He looked around in surprise. "Isn't anyone else here, either?"

"No!" Robby answered. "We're all alone, too!"

"Gosh, did you have supper?" Stewie put in. "We hardly had anything in our ice box. We're starved!"

"We just had some bread and butter," Bruce answered. He suddenly realized how hungry he was. He wondered if Mrs. Fowler had made anything for dinner.

He went into the kitchen and opened the ice box. There was plenty of milk and some orange juice but they didn't want that. There was also a big, green bowl with a plate on top of it. He lifted the plate— and saw spaghetti and meat balls!

"That must be for dinner," he said to Frankie who was peering over his shoulder. "I guess we could put it into a pot and heat it."

"Oh, yes, let's do that!" Frankie exclaimed eagerly.

Bruce found a big pot and emptied the spaghetti

131

into it. Then he put a light under it on the stove.

"We'll eat on the kitchen table," he said. "Robby! Come on and help," he called.

They were just about ready to sit down and eat when the telephone rang.

"Dad! It must be Dad!" Bruce said running to the phone. But when he lifted the receiver he was disappointed again.

"Hello, Bruce? This is Mrs. Dickerson. I've been wondering how you've been getting on in this storm. Did your father get home all right?"

"No, Dad's not here yet. He telephoned a while ago, saying he'd be here—"

"Well, if you need anything, don't hesitate to call me. This certainly is some blizzard! Good night—"

Bruce stood there as the phone clicked in his ear. It suddenly came to him that Mrs. Dickerson thought Mrs. Fowler was here with them. Should he call her back and tell her that they were alone? But she didn't like Frankie and Stewie. The Dickerson kids weren't allowed near them! No—it would be better to stay on here. And they were all hungry—ready to eat now!

It was fun, in a way almost like a little party, as they all sat around the table. The spaghetti and

132

meat balls were steaming hot and they had bread, butter and milk with them.

"Say, this is good!" Frankie said. "Can I have some more?"

"Well, just a little bit more," Bruce said. "We've got to save some for my father and Mrs. Fowler."

Afterwards everyone put his dish in the sink and they went into the living room. They pressed their faces against the window pane, looking for some sign of their parents. But the world was just a mass of whiteness, without a single person or car on the street.

"Let's play something!" Frankie said. "Let's play cowboys and Indians. You little kids be the bad guys and I'll tie you up."

"I don't want to be tied up," Robby protested.

"Well, I'll just tie Stewie. Do you have some rope?" he asked Bruce.

"There are some pieces in my room—"

Frankie ran into the room. He soon had his brother on the floor and was tying up his hands and feet. Stewie was patient about it for a little while but then he cried, "Untie me! I want to get up!"

"No, stay down there. If I untie you, you'll go over to the enemy—"

133

"I don't feel like playing this," Stewie cried. "I don't like it now. I want to get up!"

"Go on, untie him," Bruce said to Frankie.

"Why should I? I don't feel like it. I want to tie somebody else." Frankie started toward Robby with another piece of rope.

"I don't want to be tied at all!" Robby ran to Bruce. "Don't let him tie me!"

Bruce reached out and tried to pull the rope from Frankie. "Give me that!" he cried, but Frankie pushed at him, almost knocking him down.

"You can't come in here and start a fight!" he said. He started for Frankie, but he darted away, running into the living room.

"Come on, catch me if you can!" Frankie seemed to think this was great fun. "Let's have a real chase."

"Listen, we're not going to chase around and wreck the house!" Bruce said. "I let you in here but not to make trouble!"

"Go on, catch me! You're scared to catch me!" Frankie ran into the hallway again. Bruce didn't even bother to follow him until he heard a loud, twanging sound!

He knew what that was. He hurried into Mrs. Fowler's room and there was Frankie, holding the guitar which he must have taken down from the wall. He was plunking away at the strings.

"That's not yours. It's not ours either—it belongs to Mrs. Fowler. You'd better leave it alone before you break it."

"I won't break it. I like it!" Frankie was sitting in Mrs. Fowler's chair, leaning back on it as he twanged at the guitar strings still harder.

"Put that back, Frankie!" Bruce came nearer to him, reaching out for the guitar.

"I'm not hurting it. Listen to me sing. I'm the Singing Cowboy. Ladies and gentlemen, my next song will be, blang—blang—twang—twang—" He made silly noises. He was pulling at the guitar strings, leaning back on the chair—and suddenly—the chair went over!

Bruce didn't know whether to laugh or not. But he heard a sound he didn't like—and he saw that a string had snapped loose on the guitar.

"I didn't mean to do that," Frankie said, scrambling to his feet. "Maybe I can fix it." He reached for the guitar again.

"You never mean to do anything!" Bruce grabbed the guitar first. He was suddenly mad, his eyes blazing with fury. "Pick up that chair!" His voice was firm, sounding more like a grown-up's than his own.

135

Frankie was so startled by it that he picked up the chair, looking at Bruce in bewilderment.

"Now you listen to me." Bruce came close to Frankie. "If you want to stay here another minute, you've got to act better! You get back into my room and untie Stewie. And then you sit down and play or something without getting into trouble! Because if you don't do that, you're going right out into the snow and you can freeze for all I care!"

"Oh, all right. I didn't mean to do anything wrong!" Frankie grumbled. He went back into the boys' room, Bruce following him. Robby had been helping Stewie to get untied and they were almost done. Frankie bent down and finished the job.

"I've been thinking," Bruce went on. "It's getting late and way past your bedtime, Robby. I think we ought to lend Stewie some pajamas and then both of you can go to sleep while Frankie and I wait up for the grown ups."

"That's not fair!" Stewie cried. "I don't want to sleep here. I want to go home." He ran to the window. "Maybe somebody's home now." He stared through the snow. "I think there's a light in the house."

"We left a light on." Frankie stood beside Stewie.

137

"I know the number where my mother works. I'm going to call there!"

Bruce followed Frankie to the telephone. Frankie lifted the receiver off the hook and started to dial. But then he looked a bit frightened and said, "I don't hear any kind of noise at all! Do you think something's wrong with the telephone?"

Bruce came and took the phone from him. He didn't hear a sound. He dialed the operator and no sound came. He jiggled the phone and it was still quiet.

"Something must be wrong!" he said. For a moment he stood there, frightened, and he saw Robby and Stewie staring at him and looking scared, too.

"I guess the snow put the phones out of order. Anyway—what's the use of talking to anybody." He forced a smile to his lips. "They'll get here when they can."

"Sure, that's right!" He was glad to hear Frankie back him up.

"I still think you two ought to get into bed," Bruce went on to Robby and Stewie. "You don't have to sleep right away, but you'll get into less trouble if you're in bed. Go on, do as I say," he ordered Stewie firmly, looking at Frankie at the same time,

138

as if to add, "Help me get your brother to behave or you can both go!"

"Come on, do as he says!" Frankie put in.

There were grumbles from Stewie, and some from Robby too, but they both finally got into pajamas and into bed.

"You can talk awhile if you like," Bruce said. "But no wild stuff!"

"What'll we do?" Frankie asked as they started for the living room.

"Here—take some of these books—and some games—" Bruce said and then they went inside.

They started a game of checkers, sitting on the floor of the living room. Every once in a while Bruce thought he heard a car but when he went to the window there was just snow—snow—snow!

Where were Dad and Mrs. Fowler? Why didn't they even telephone? But when he went to the phone again, lifting the receiver to his ear, there was still no sound. Dad couldn't phone even if he wanted to!

"I—I'm sleepy." Frankie's mouth opened in a wide yawn. "I don't think they're coming home at all to-night."

"Why don't you stretch out on the couch there," Bruce said. "I'll give you a blanket."

139

"All right—" Frankie was on the couch quickly, lifting his feet from the floor.

"Take off your shoes," Bruce told him.

He brought two blankets, one for Frankie and one for himself on the other end of the couch.

In a very few minutes Frankie was sound asleep but Bruce lay there, his eyes tired, his mind full of thoughts.

Suppose something had happened to Dad and Mrs. Fowler. But no—they were just stuck somewhere in the snow and couldn't phone—he knew it wasn't anything worse than that. In a way he was glad Frankie and Stewie had come over—but it sure had been hard to make Frankie behave!

Bruce's eyes grew heavier. He pulled the blanket up higher. Why didn't Dad come home—he wished he would hurry—

"Bruce! Bruce!" At first he thought he was still having a dream. He had been dreaming that he was riding in the car with Dad and Robby to Grandma and Grandpa's house and it had begun to snow. So much white, falling snow— "Bruce! Bruce!"

He opened his eyes and there was Dad leaning over him.

140

"Dad! You're home!" He flung his arms around his father's neck.

Then he saw that there were other people in the room. Mrs. Fowler—and wasn't that lady Frankie and Stewie's mother? There was so much commotion—everybody seemed to be talking at once!

"We were all held up by the snow and had to wait in the hotel lobby downtown," Dad was saying. "We couldn't get through until the snow plows were able to clear the roads and they just did that a little while ago."

"The phones were out of order and we were so worried about you!" Mrs. Fowler put in.

"You're all right, Frankie, you're all right, aren't you?" his mother was saying. "The house was so cold and I was so frightened when Stewie and you weren't there. Until I found your note—"

"Bruce took good care of us," Frankie said. "We had spaghetti and meat balls for supper and he made Stewie go to sleep, too."

"Dad's home fixing the oil burner and he has it going now," Frankie's mother went on. "I knew we'd been having trouble with it and I was so worried about you boys. I—I can't go on working during the day, leaving you and Stewie alone so much—"

141

"What is it? What's the matter?" Robby and Stewie came into the room just then, looking half asleep. "Daddy—you're back!" Robby ran into his father's arms.

"What a time for you children to be up!" Mrs. Fowler said, putting her arms around Bruce. "I'm so glad you found the spaghetti in the ice box—"

"There's some left for Dad and you," Bruce said. He didn't know why, but Mrs. Fowler hugged him even tighter at that.

"Why don't you let Stewie spend the rest of the night here, instead of bothering to dress him," Dad asked the boys' mother. "Bruce can stay out here on the sofa. He'll be all right."

"I suppose that is the best idea," Stewie's mother agreed. "But you put your boots and coat on, Frankie, and come along—"

Bruce got into his pajamas while Mrs. Fowler made up the living room sofa with sheets and blankets.

"Is it still snowing?" Bruce asked. "It looks as if there had never been so much snow in the world!"

"It was a pretty big blizzard all right," Dad said. "But I think it's letting up a bit now." He tucked Bruce under the covers on the sofa. "Sleep as late as you can and I'll see you in the morning. There won't be any schools or businesses open tomorrow, I'm sure of that."

It was easy to fall asleep this time—knowing that Dad was home!

Bruce slept later than he ever had but when he did wake up the next morning, he could hardly get dressed fast enough. He ate breakfast quickly and hurried outdoors.

How beautiful it was outside, snow pure and white as far as you could see. Some people were outdoors shoveling their walks. Bruce ran to the garage and found one of their shovels.

It was fun digging the shovel in the snow, trying to clear the front walk. The snow came up in great, big, soft chunks that Bruce was able to toss aside easily. Soon Robby was out, shoveling beside him, and they had quite a path cleared by the time the front door opened and Dad appeared.

"Can I join you out there?" Dad asked. "I'll get myself a shovel."

"You can take this one," Robby said. "I want to play with Phil—"

He handed Dad a shovel that was much too small. Both Bruce and his father looked at the little shovel and laughed. Dad went to the garage and came back with a man-sized shovel. Then he started to dig near Bruce.

"You've certainly gotten a lot done." Dad admired the path behind Bruce. "You're really getting big and strong!"

"I guess I am!" Bruce dug still harder.

Dad paused a moment, looking at Bruce. "You're getting strong in lots of ways, Bruce. Do you know how proud I am about the way you came through last night?"

"Last night?" Bruce looked up. "What did I do?"

"Well, some kids would have gone into a real panic left alone in a snowstorm like that. But you managed to see that everyone had some supper and that Robby and Stewie went to bed and that Frankie didn't go wild. Knowing Frankie, that couldn't have been too easy."

"Well, it wasn't so hard," Bruce answered. "He—he started to fool around with Mrs. Fowler's guitar—and when he broke a string on it—I got real mad. I just told him to watch out or he'd have to go—"

"Once you would have gotten into trouble with him," Dad went on. "You know, Bruce, sometimes from having a lot of problems—the way we do trying to manage without Mom—you grow stronger.

144

You have to grow stronger in order to be able to pull through all that happens to you."

Bruce paused at his shoveling and listened to Dad.

"Of course it isn't better living the way we do—without Mom," Dad added softly. "But good things can come out of it. I'm just trying to say that I'm proud of you—that's all!"

Bruce couldn't help grinning happily, as he went on shoveling with Dad.